DRAGON PUNCHER

BY JAMES KOCHALKA

Other books by
James Kochalka

Johnny Boo: The Best Little Ghost in the World
Johnny Boo: Twinkle Power
Johnny Boo & the Happy Apples
Johnny Boo and the Mean Little Boy
Pinky & Stinky
Monkey Vs. Robot
Monkey Vs. Robot and the Crystal of Power
Peanutbutter & Jeremy's Best Book Ever
Squirrelly Gray

ISBN: 978-1-60309-057-5
1.Children's Books
2. Dragons
3. Graphic Novels

Dragon Puncher © 2010 James Kochalka.
Published by Top Shelf Productions, PO Box 1282, Marietta,
GA 30061-1282, USA. Publishers: Brett Warnock and Chris
Staros. Top Shelf Productions® and the Top Shelf logo
are registered trademarks of Top Shelf Productions, Inc.
All Rights Reserved. No part of this publication may be re-
produced without permission, except for small excerpts for
purposes of review. Visit our online catalog at www.top-
shelfcomix.com. First Printing, July 2010. Printed in China

Photographed and drawn
in Burlington, Vermont.

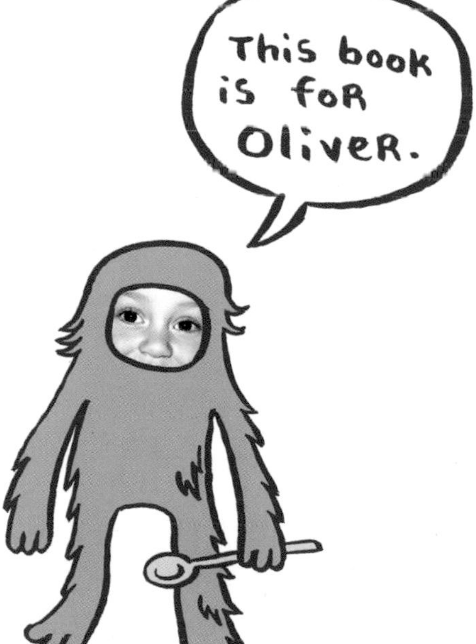
This book is for Oliver.

Here we go!

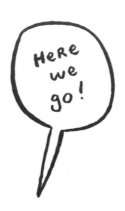

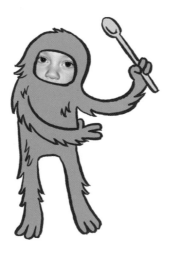

CHAPTER ONE

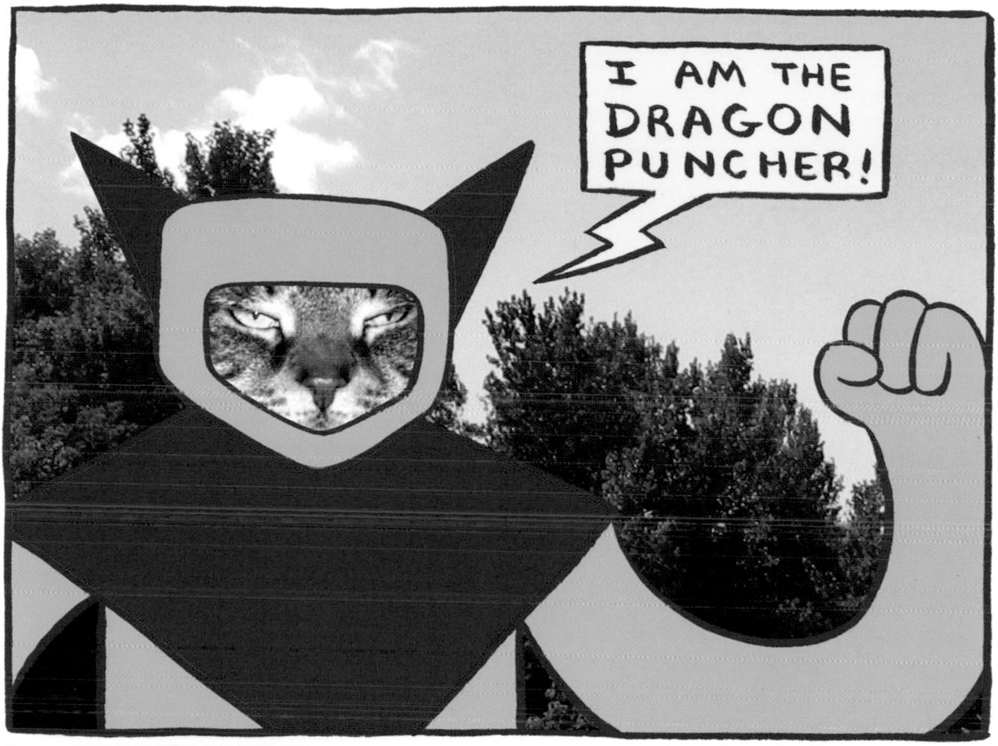
I AM THE DRAGON PUNCHER!

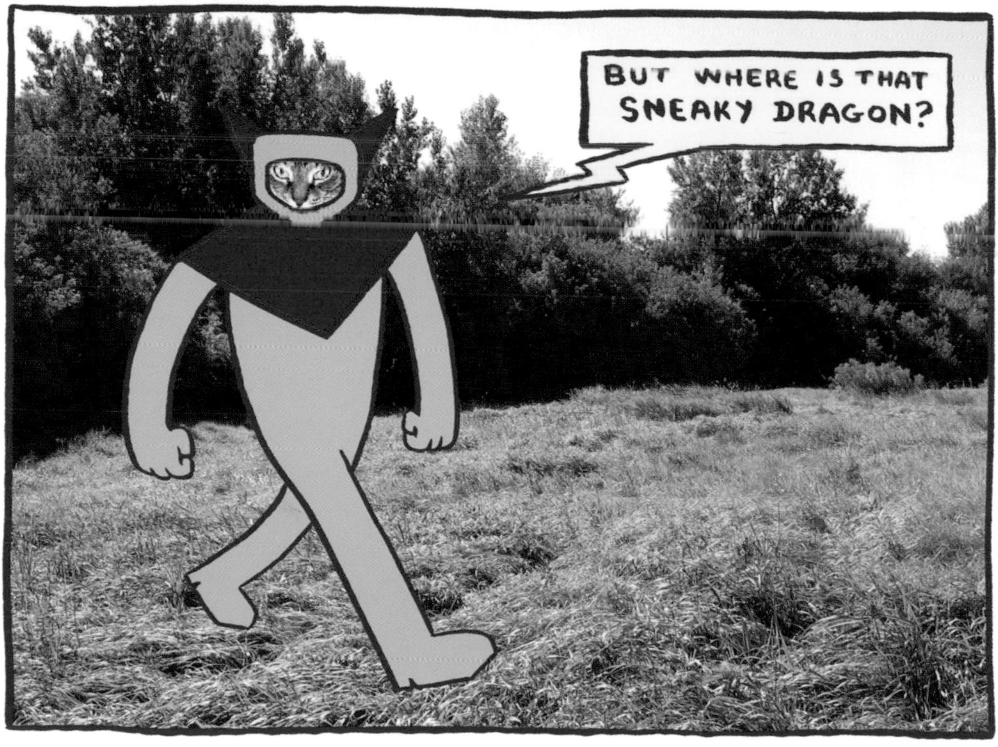
BUT WHERE IS THAT SNEAKY DRAGON?

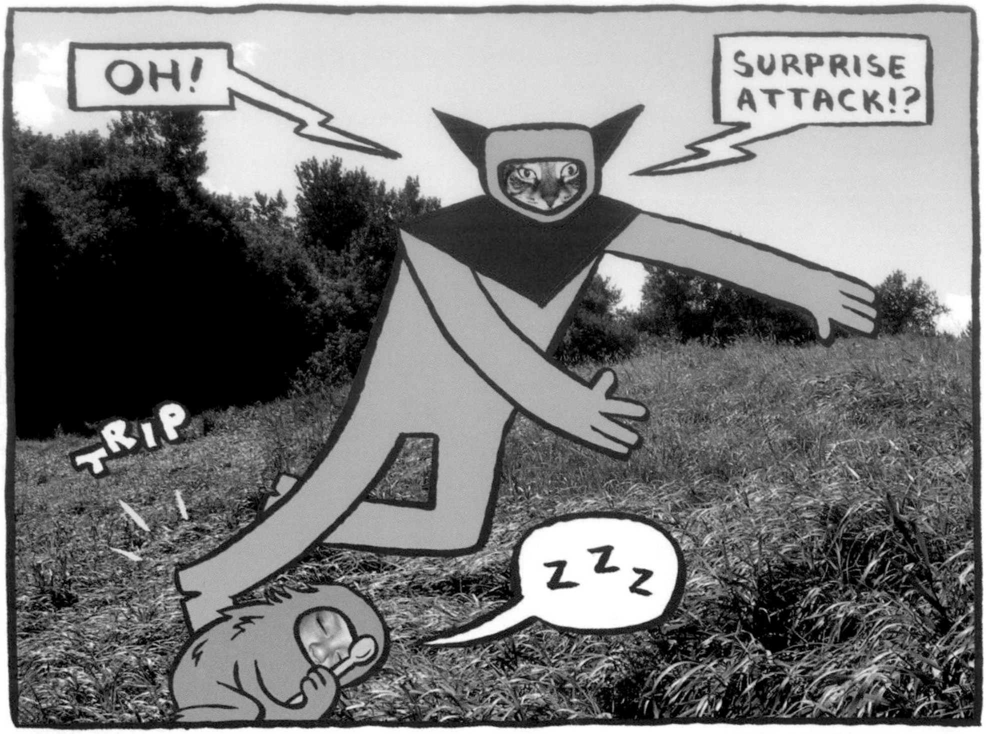
OH!
SURPRISE ATTACK!?
TRIP
Z Z Z

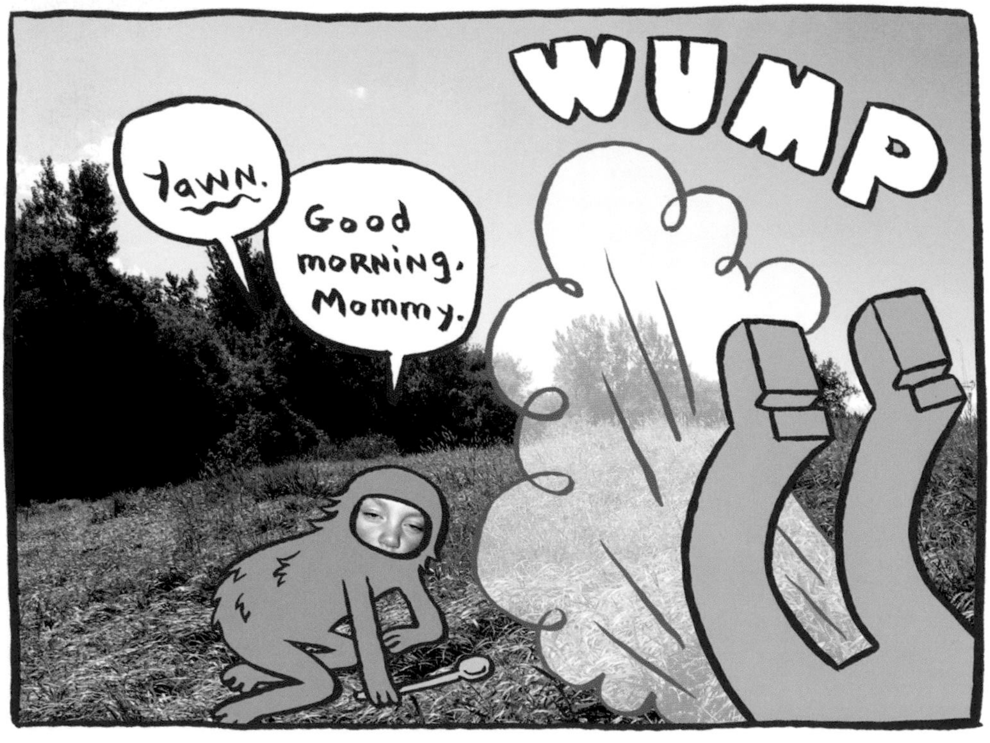
WUMP
Yawn.
Good morning, Mommy.

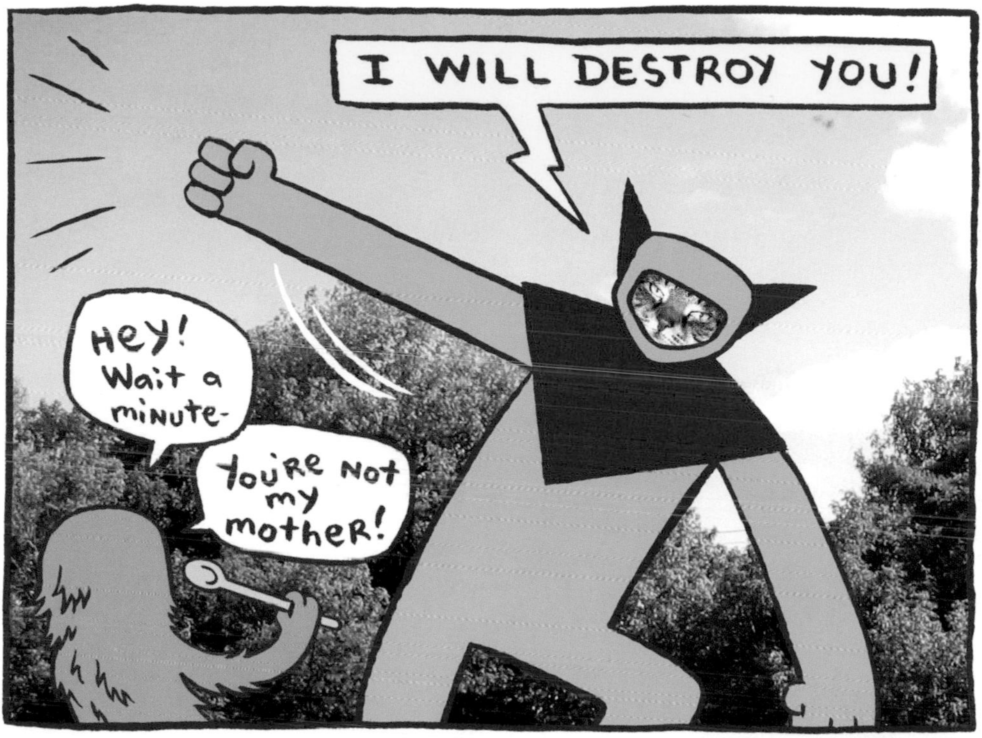
I WILL DESTROY YOU!
Hey! Wait a minute-
You're not my mother!

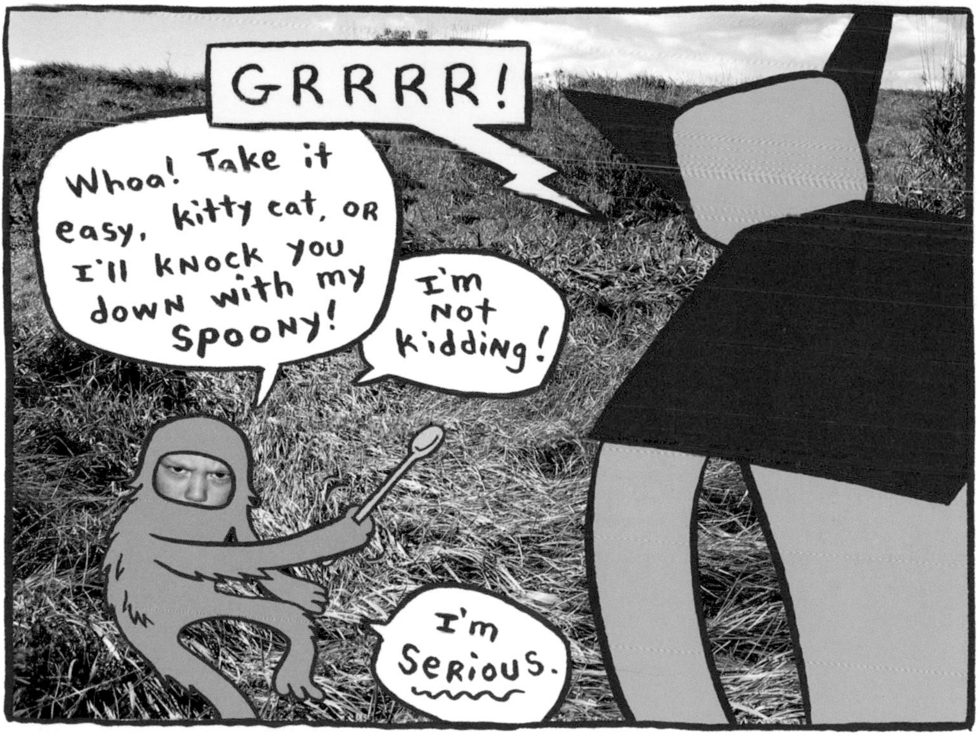
GRRRR!
Whoa! Take it easy, kitty cat, or I'll knock you down with my spoony!
I'm not kidding!
I'm serious.

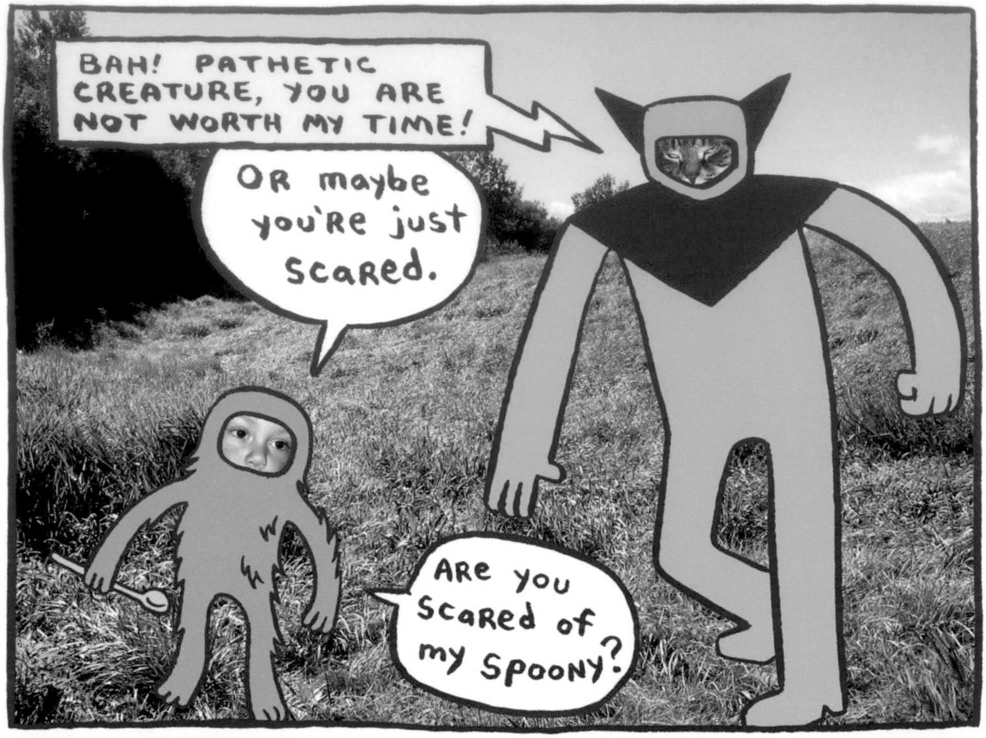
BAH! PATHETIC CREATURE, YOU ARE NOT WORTH MY TIME!
OR maybe you're just scared.
Are you scared of my spoony?

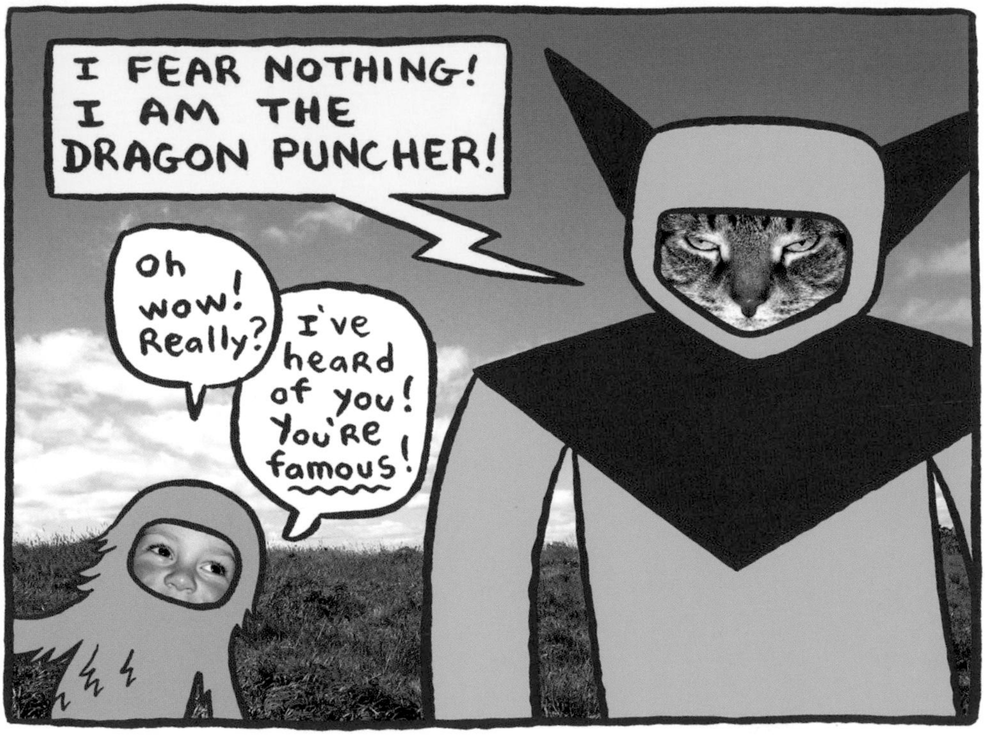
I FEAR NOTHING! I AM THE DRAGON PUNCHER!
Oh wow! Really?
I've heard of you! You're famous!

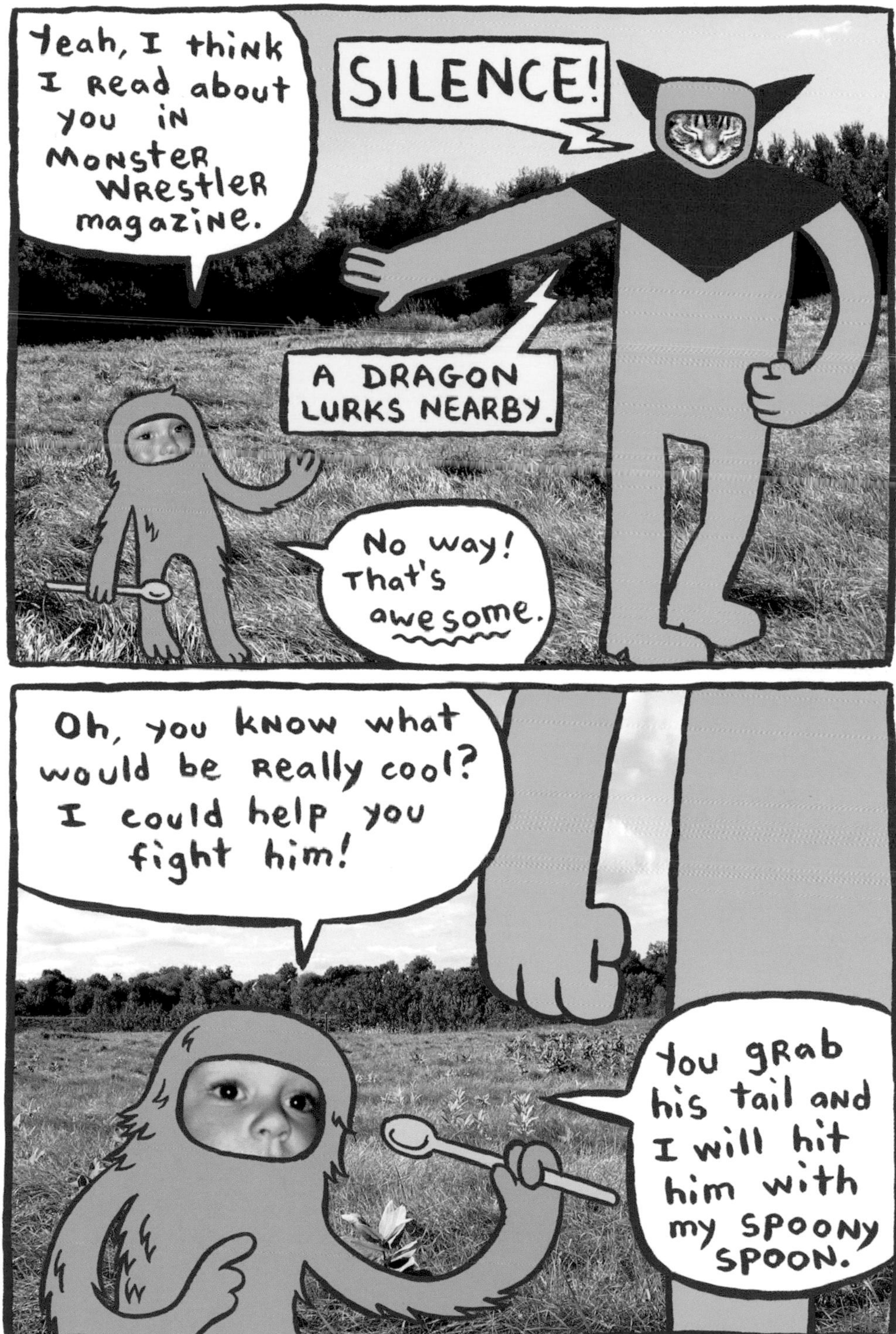
Yeah, I think I read about you in Monster Wrestler magazine.
SILENCE!
A DRAGON LURKS NEARBY.
No way! That's awesome.
Oh, you know what would be really cool? I could help you fight him!
You grab his tail and I will hit him with my spoony spoon.

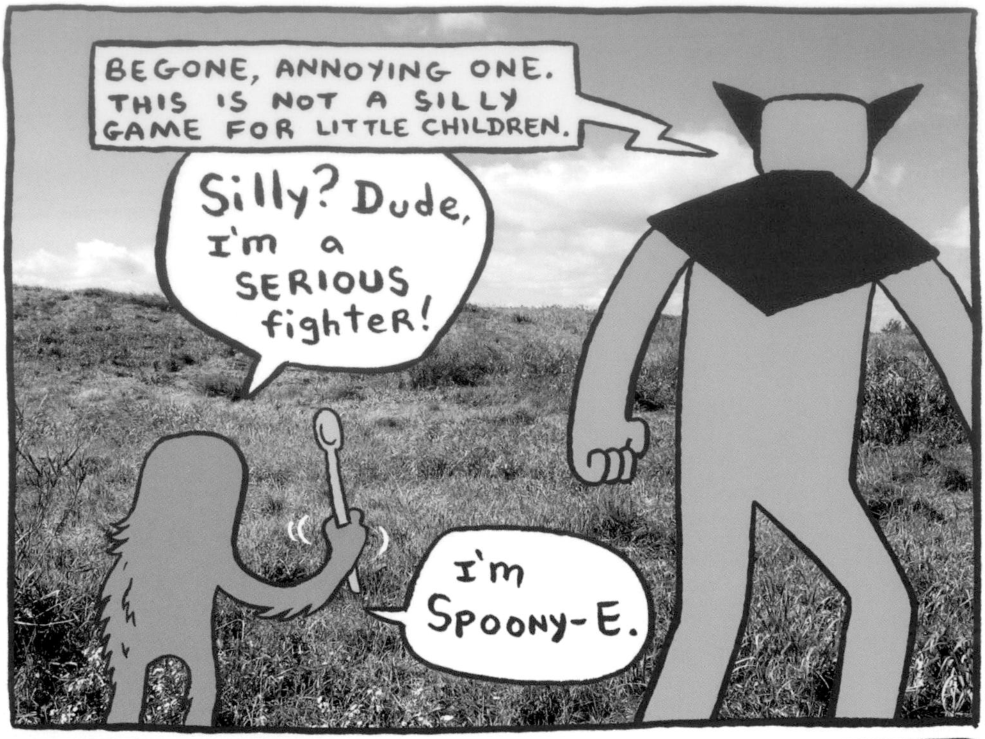
BEGONE, ANNOYING ONE. THIS IS NOT A SILLY GAME FOR LITTLE CHILDREN.
Silly? Dude, I'm a SERIOUS fighter!
I'm Spoony-E.

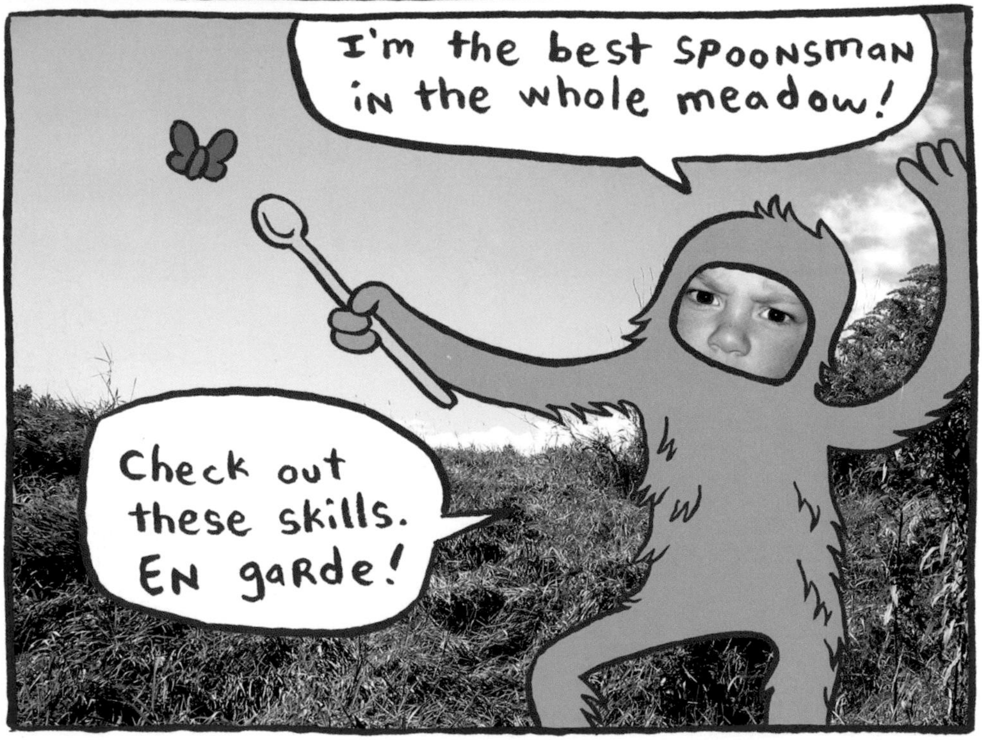
I'm the best spoonsman in the whole meadow!
Check out these skills. En garde!

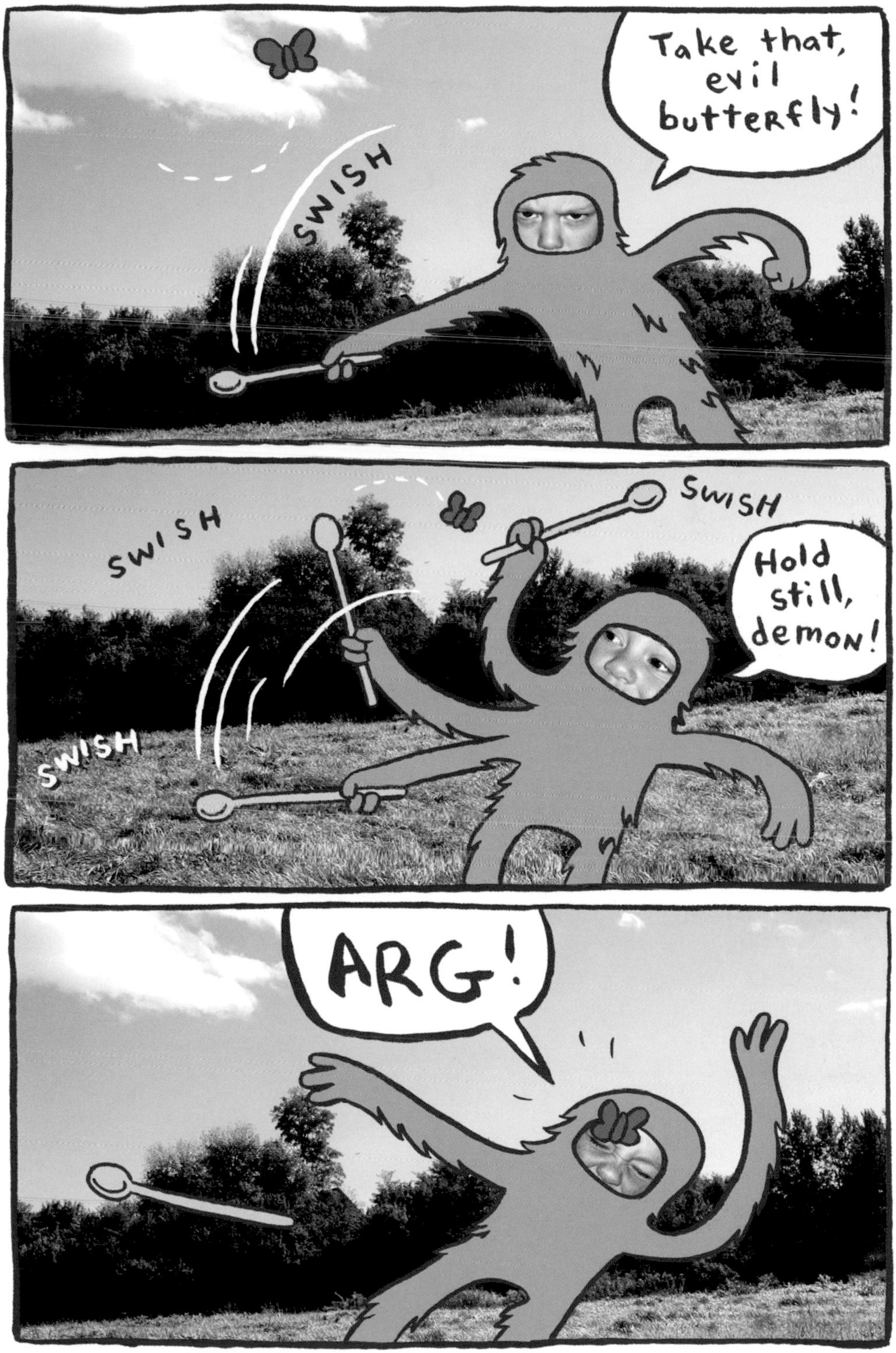
Take that, evil butterfly!
SWISH
SWISH
SWISH
Hold still, demon!
SWISH
ARG!

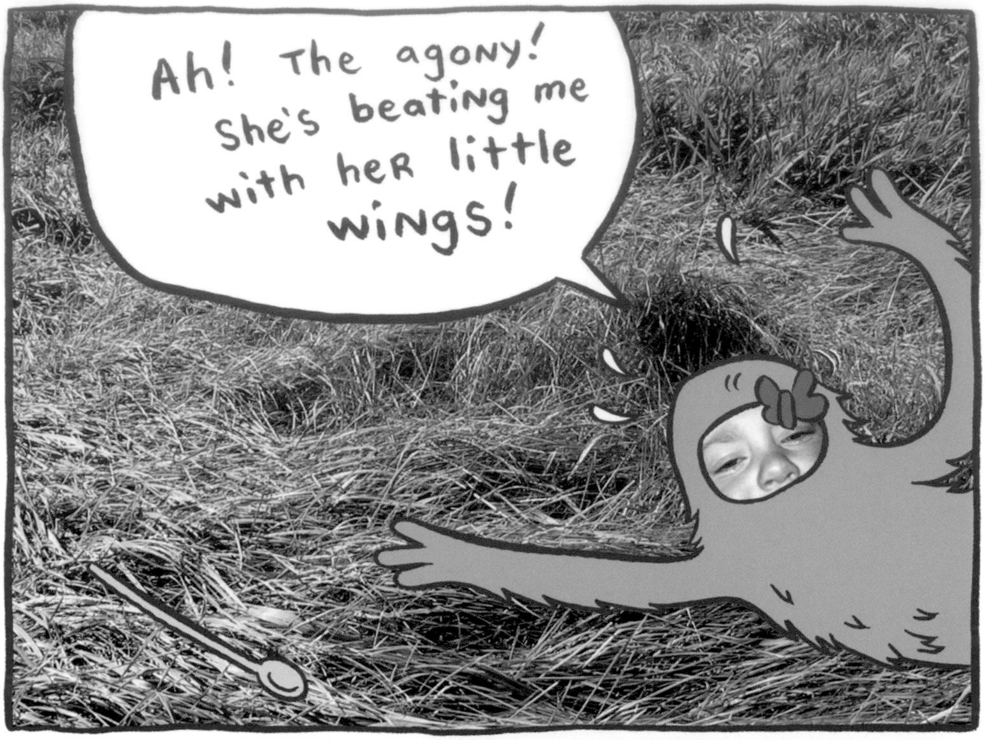
Ah! The agony! She's beating me with her little wings!

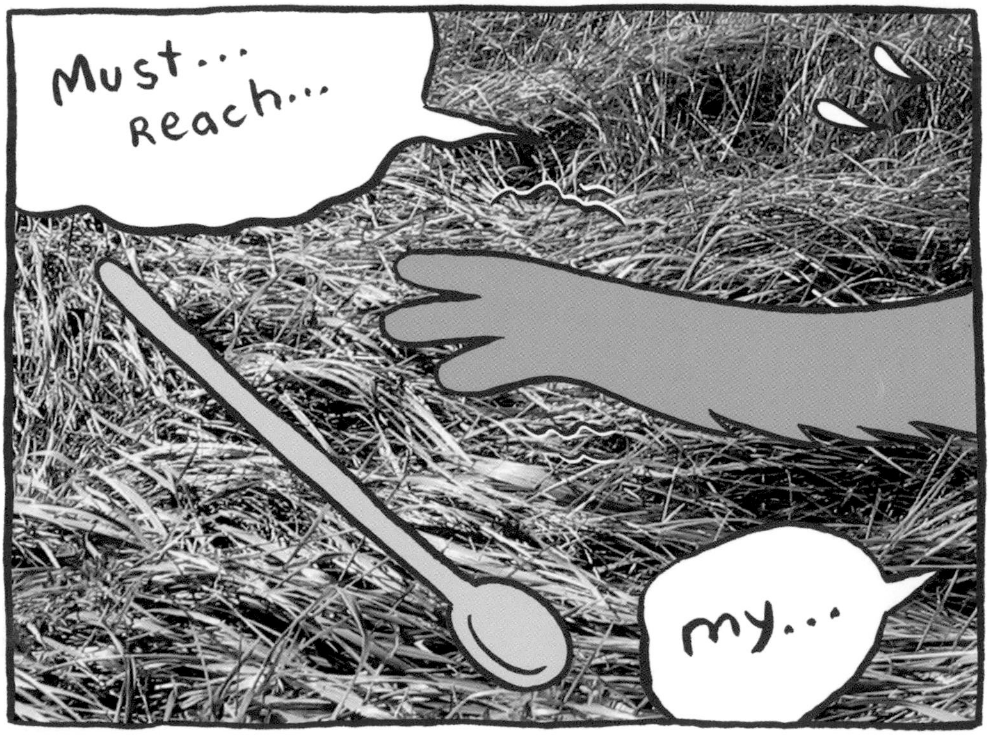
Must... reach...
my...

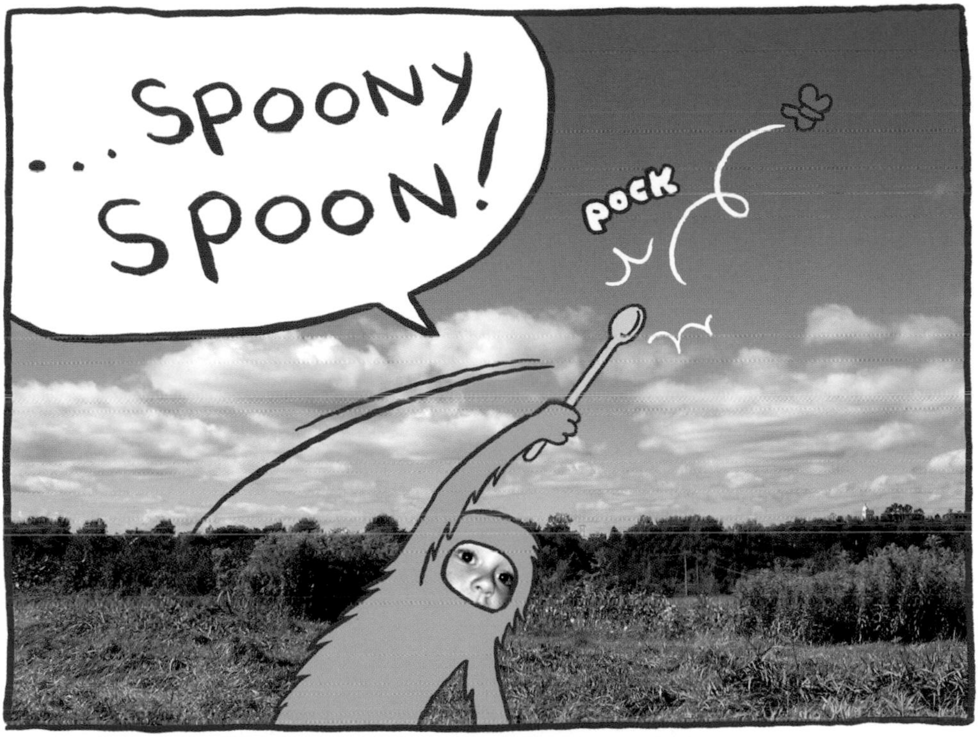
...SPOONY SPOON!
POCK

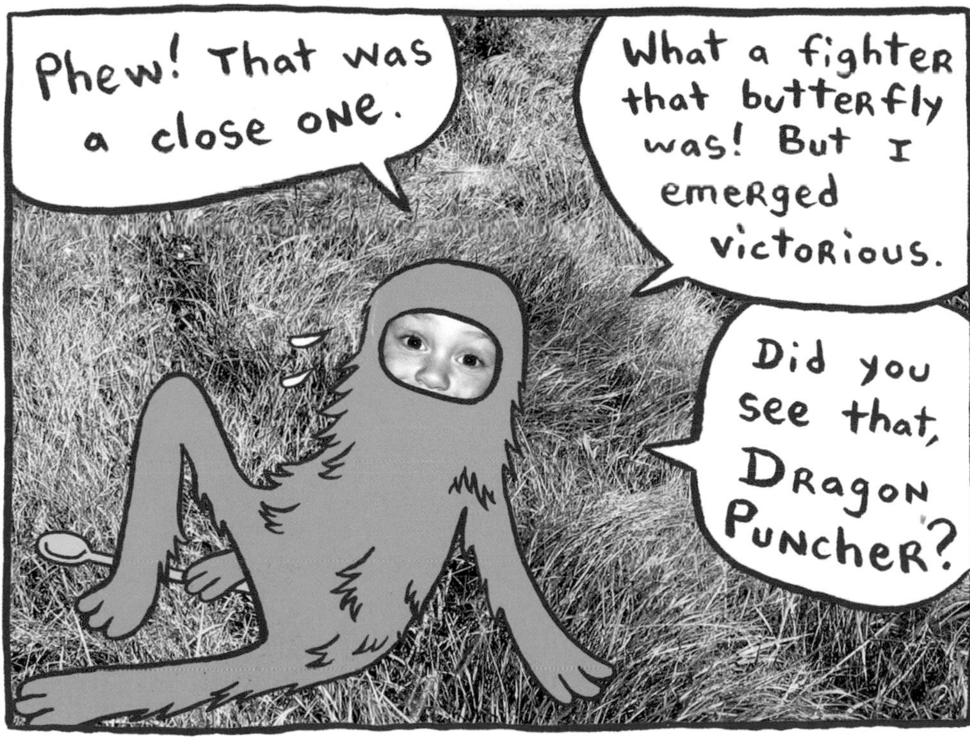
Phew! That was a close one.
What a fighter that butterfly was! But I emerged victorious.
Did you see that, DRAGON PUNCHER?

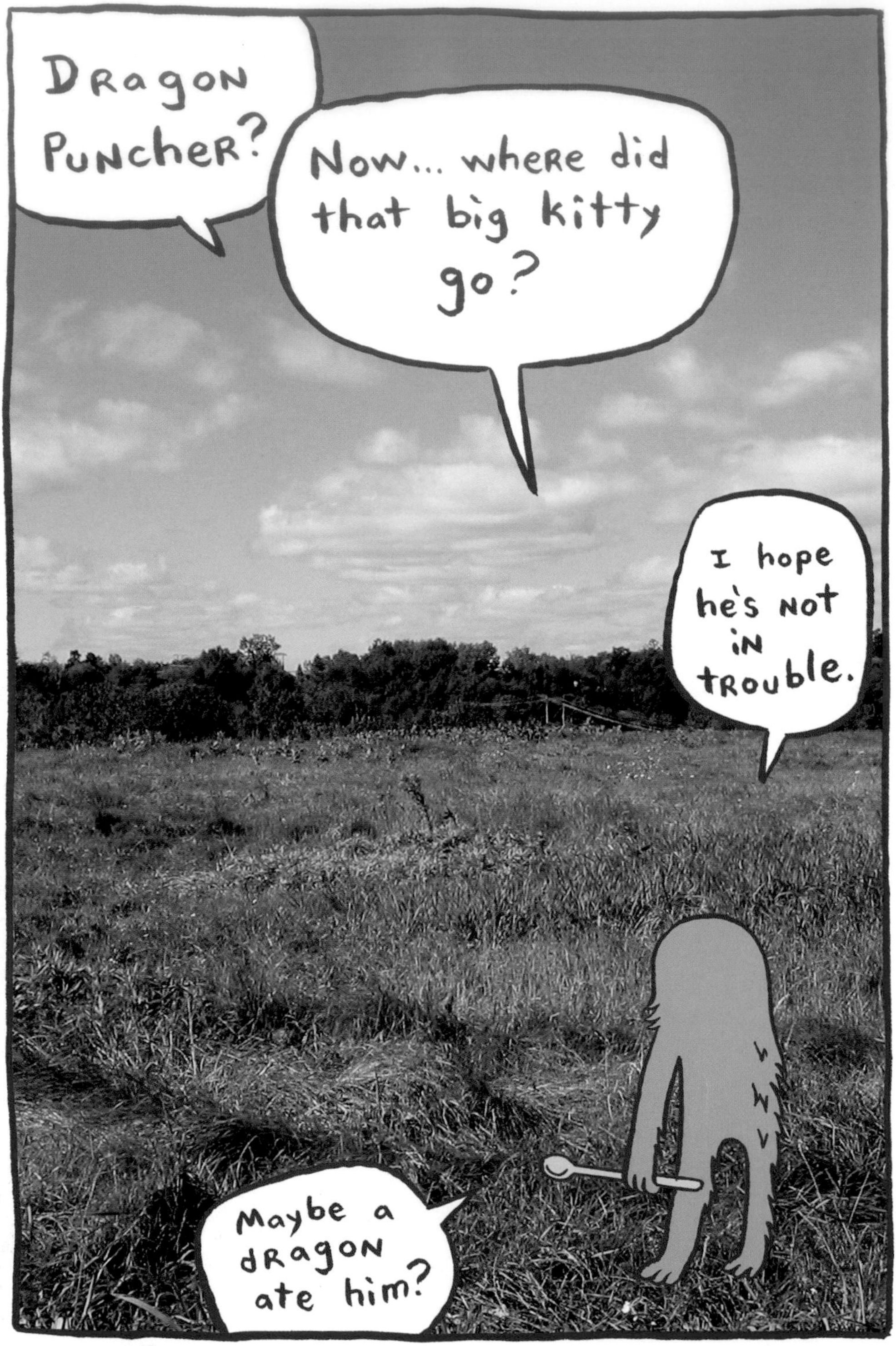
Dragon Puncher?
Now... where did that big kitty go?
I hope he's not in trouble.
Maybe a dragon ate him?

CHAPTER TWO:

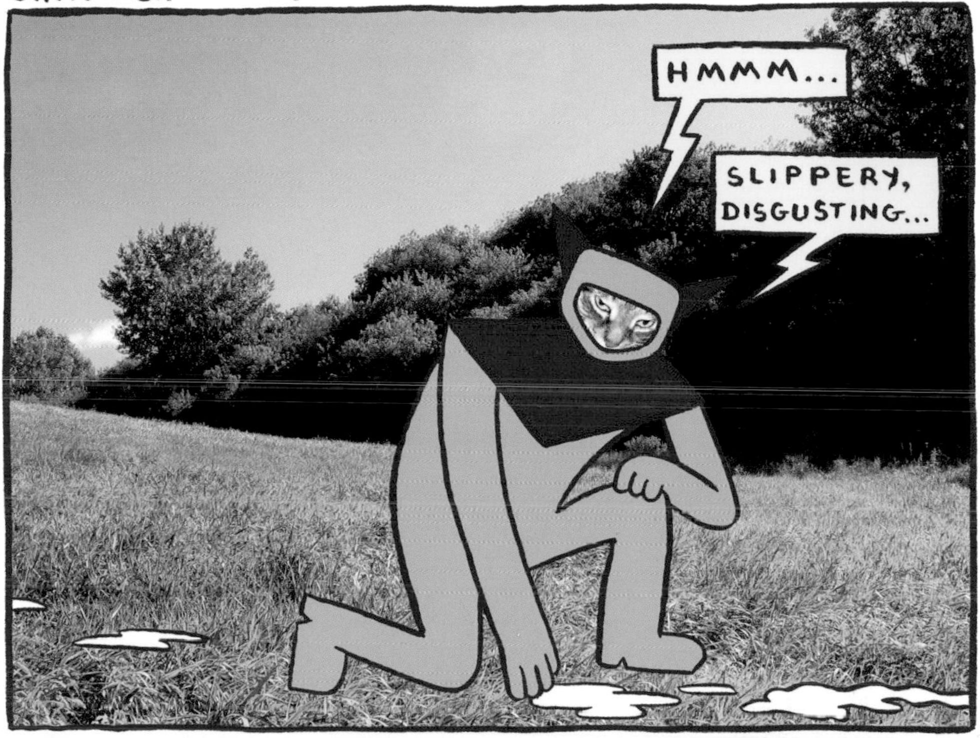
HMMM...
SLIPPERY, DISGUSTING...

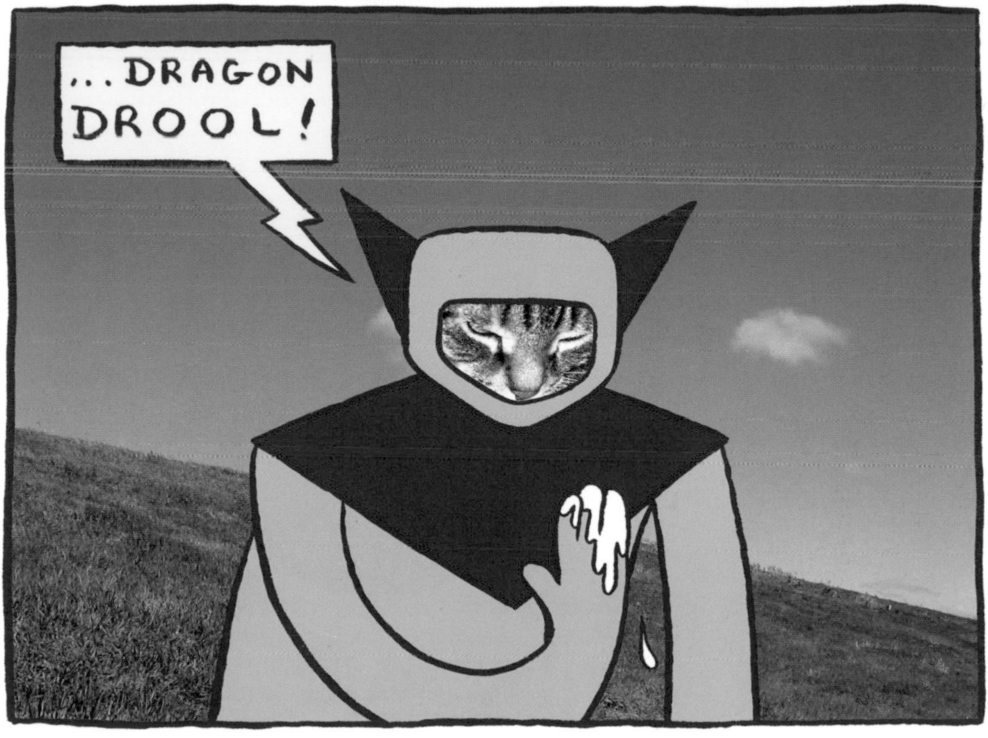
...DRAGON DROOL!

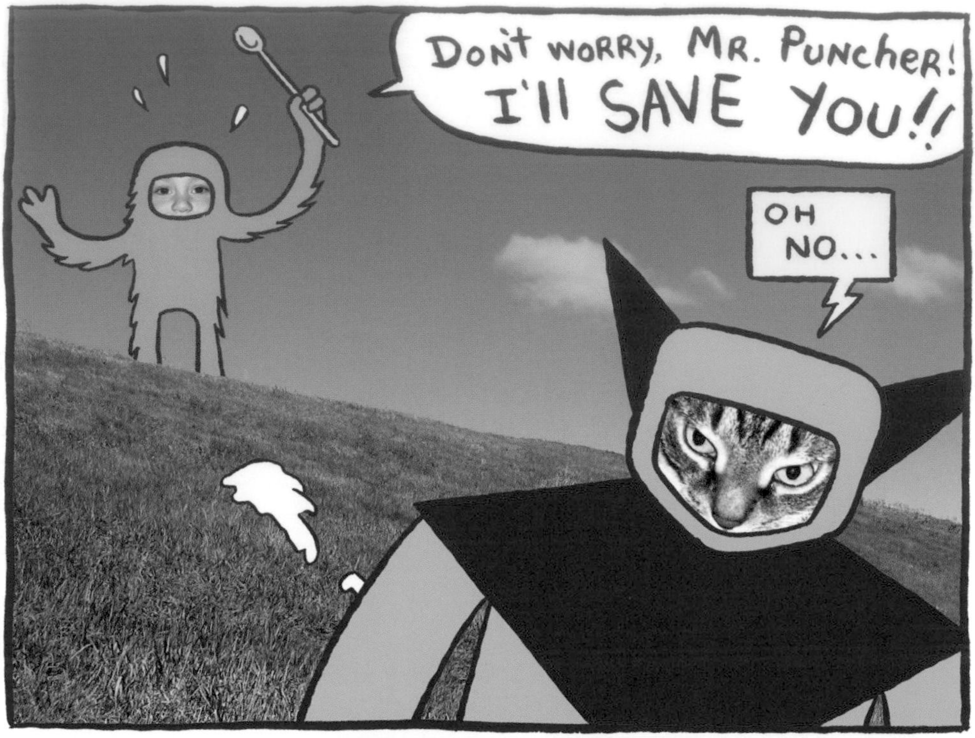
Don't worry, Mr. Puncher! I'll SAVE You!!
OH NO...

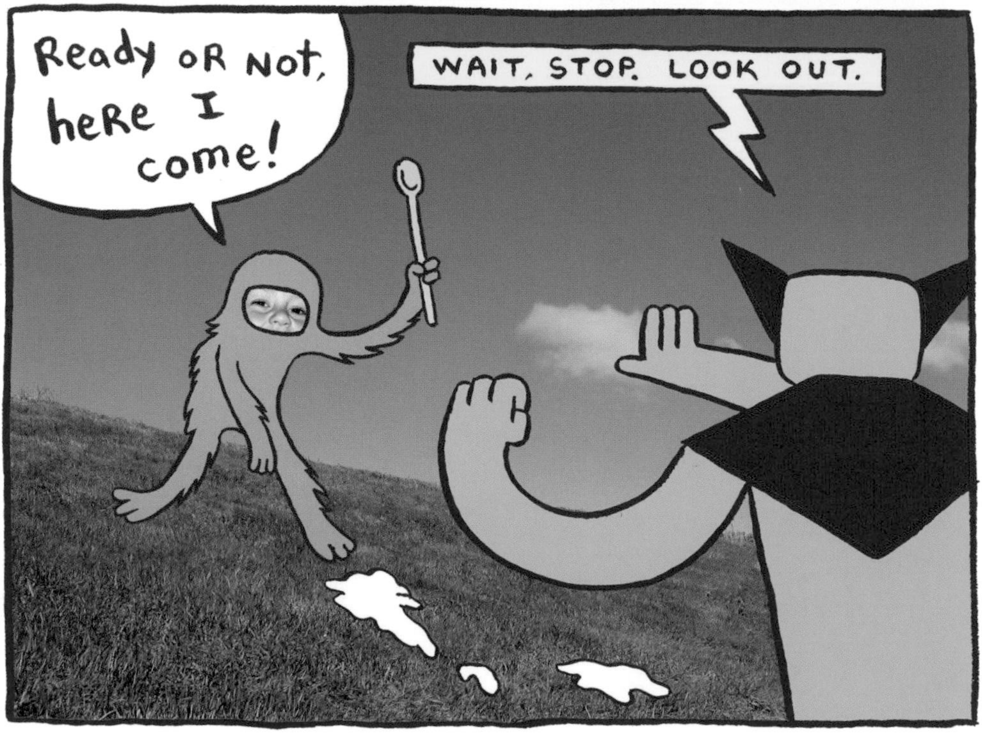
Ready or not, here I come!
WAIT, STOP. LOOK OUT.

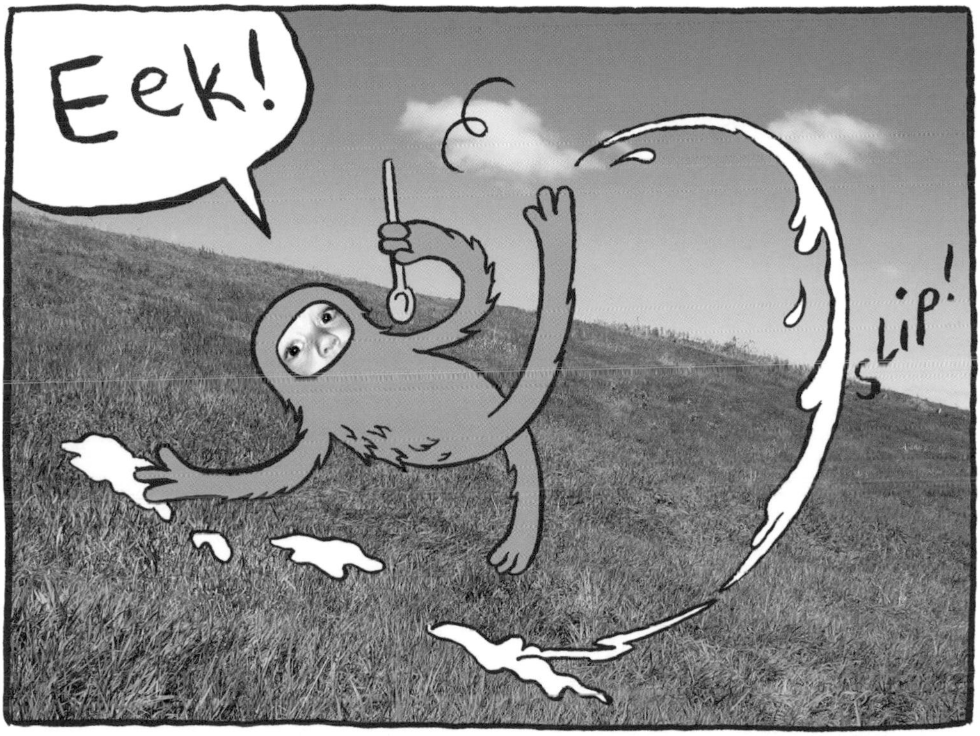
Eek!
SLIP!
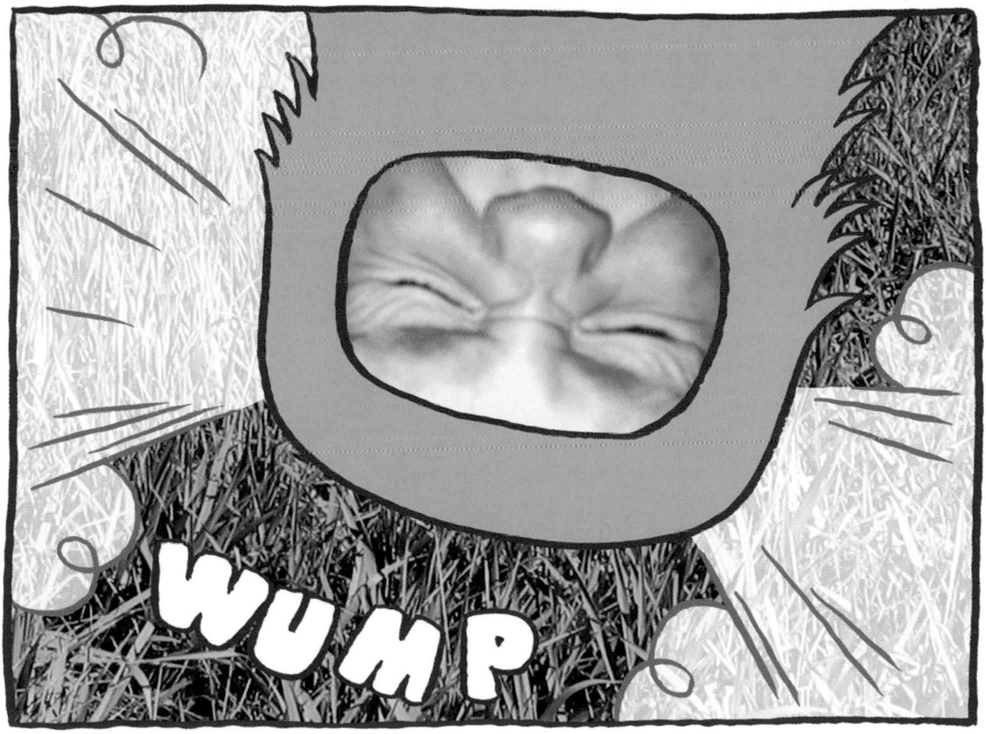
WUMP

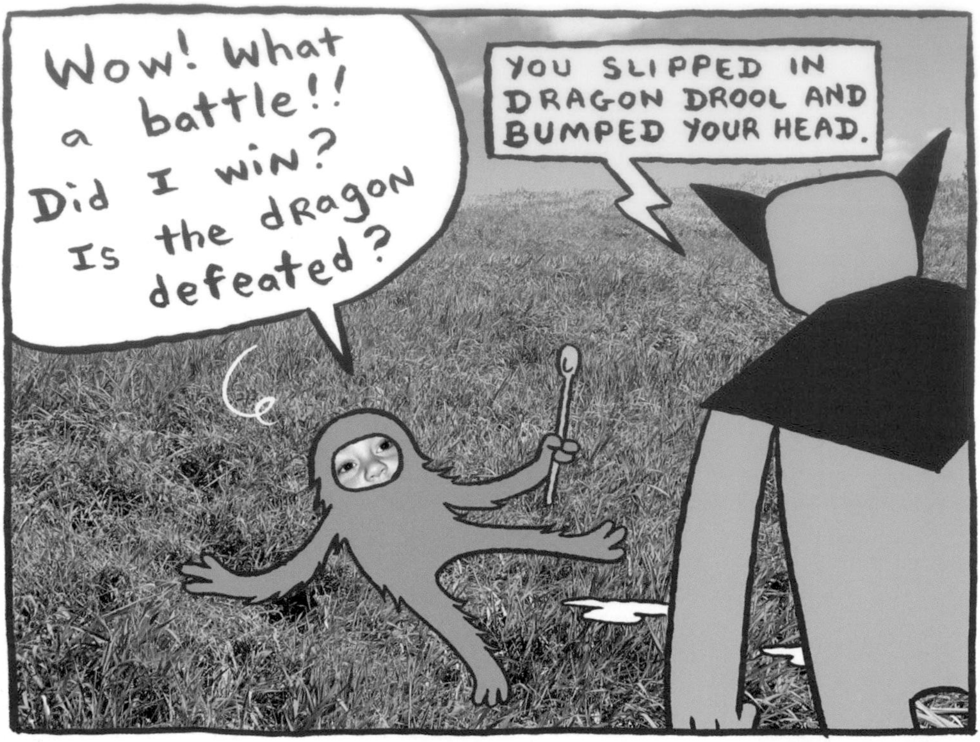
Wow! What a battle!! Did I win? Is the dragon defeated?
YOU SLIPPED IN DRAGON DROOL AND BUMPED YOUR HEAD.

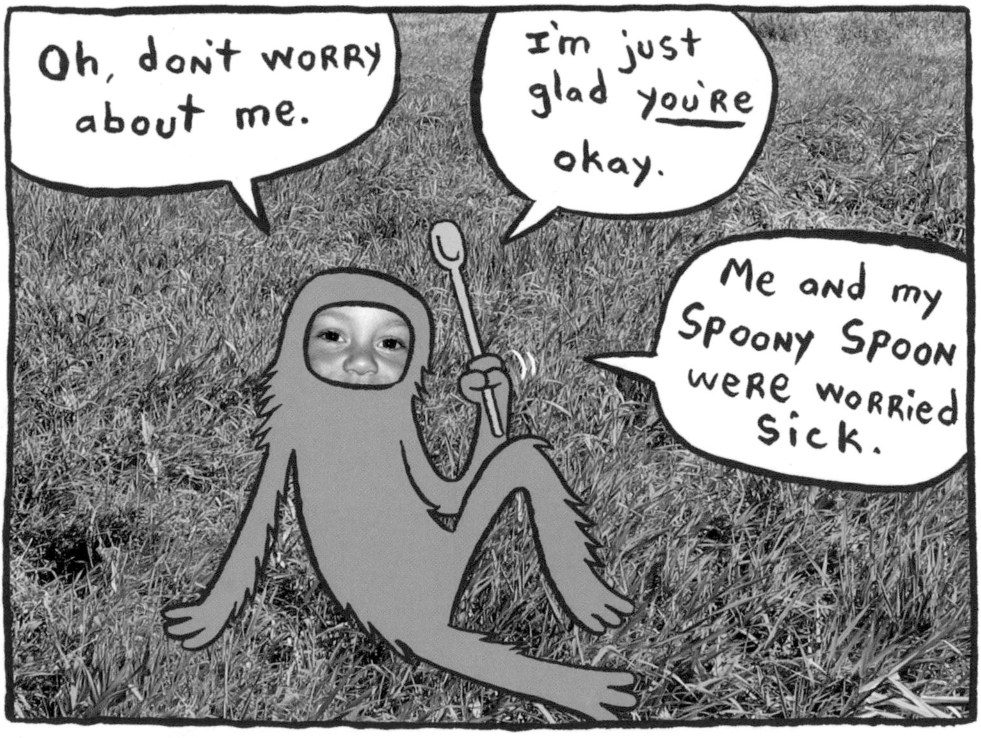
Oh, don't WORRY about me.
I'm just glad you're okay.
Me and my Spoony Spoon were worried sick.

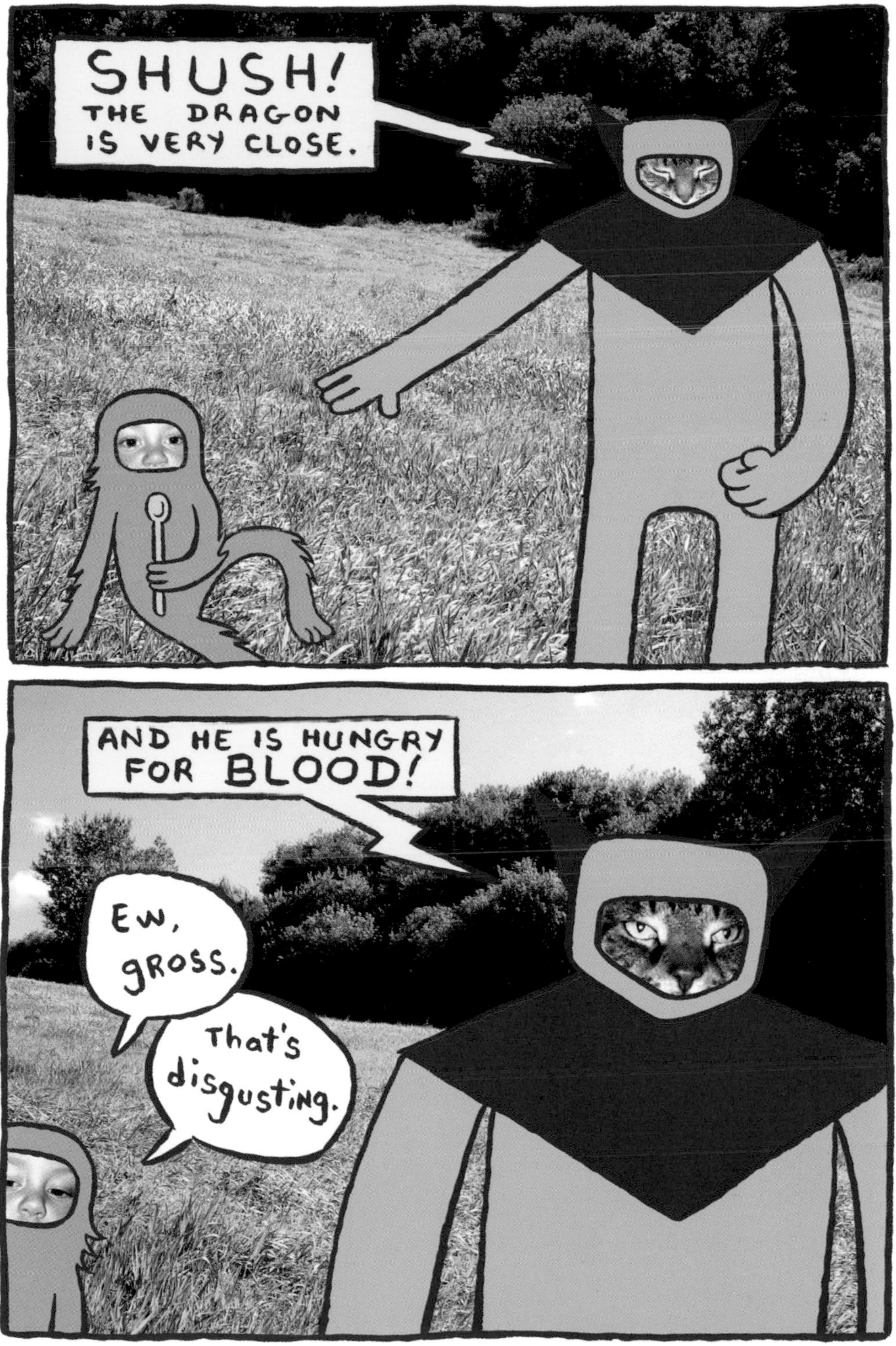
SHUSH! THE DRAGON IS VERY CLOSE.
AND HE IS HUNGRY FOR BLOOD!
Ew, gross.
That's disgusting.

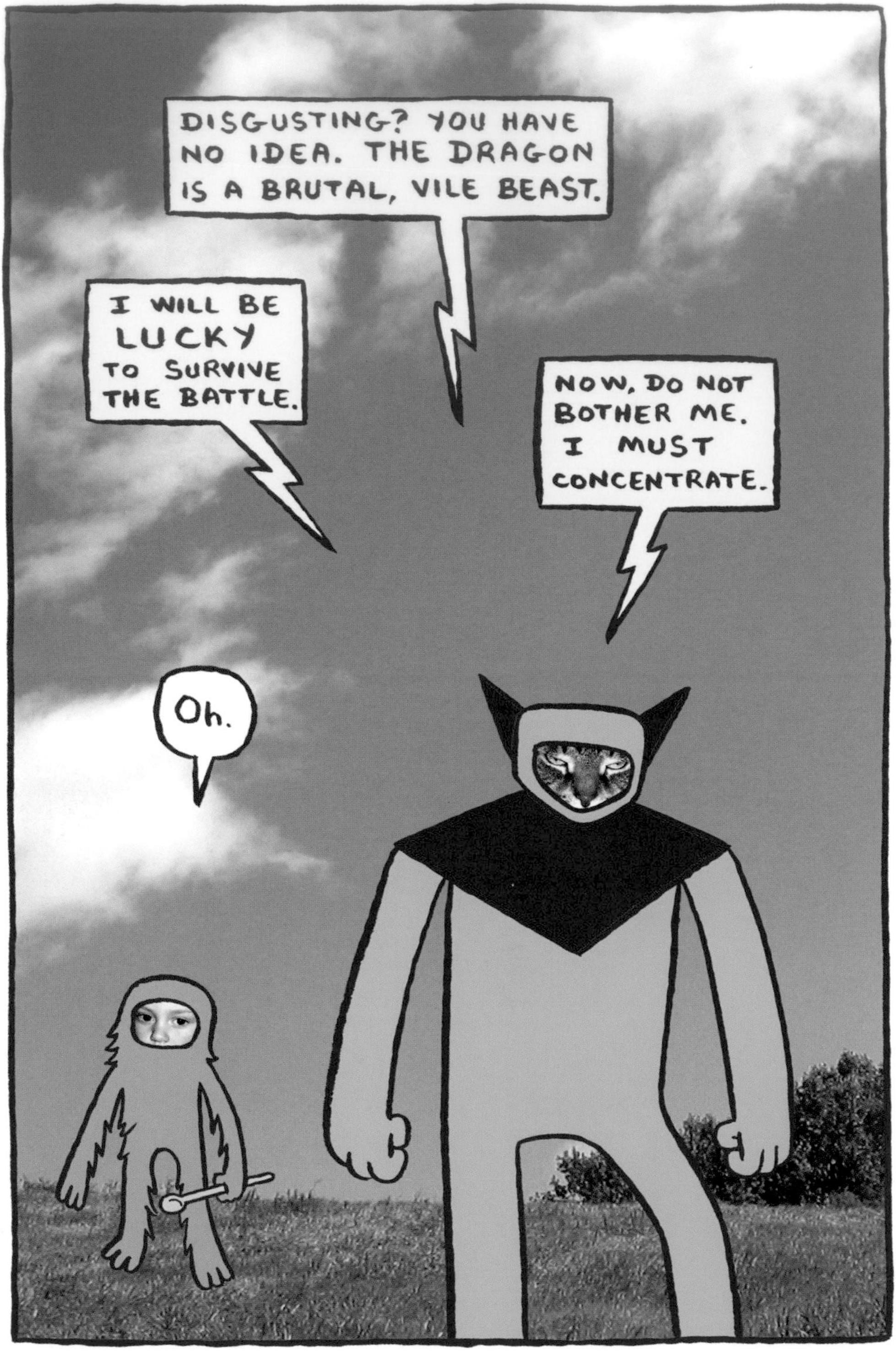
DISGUSTING? YOU HAVE NO IDEA. THE DRAGON IS A BRUTAL, VILE BEAST.
I WILL BE LUCKY TO SURVIVE THE BATTLE.
NOW, DO NOT BOTHER ME. I MUST CONCENTRATE.
Oh.

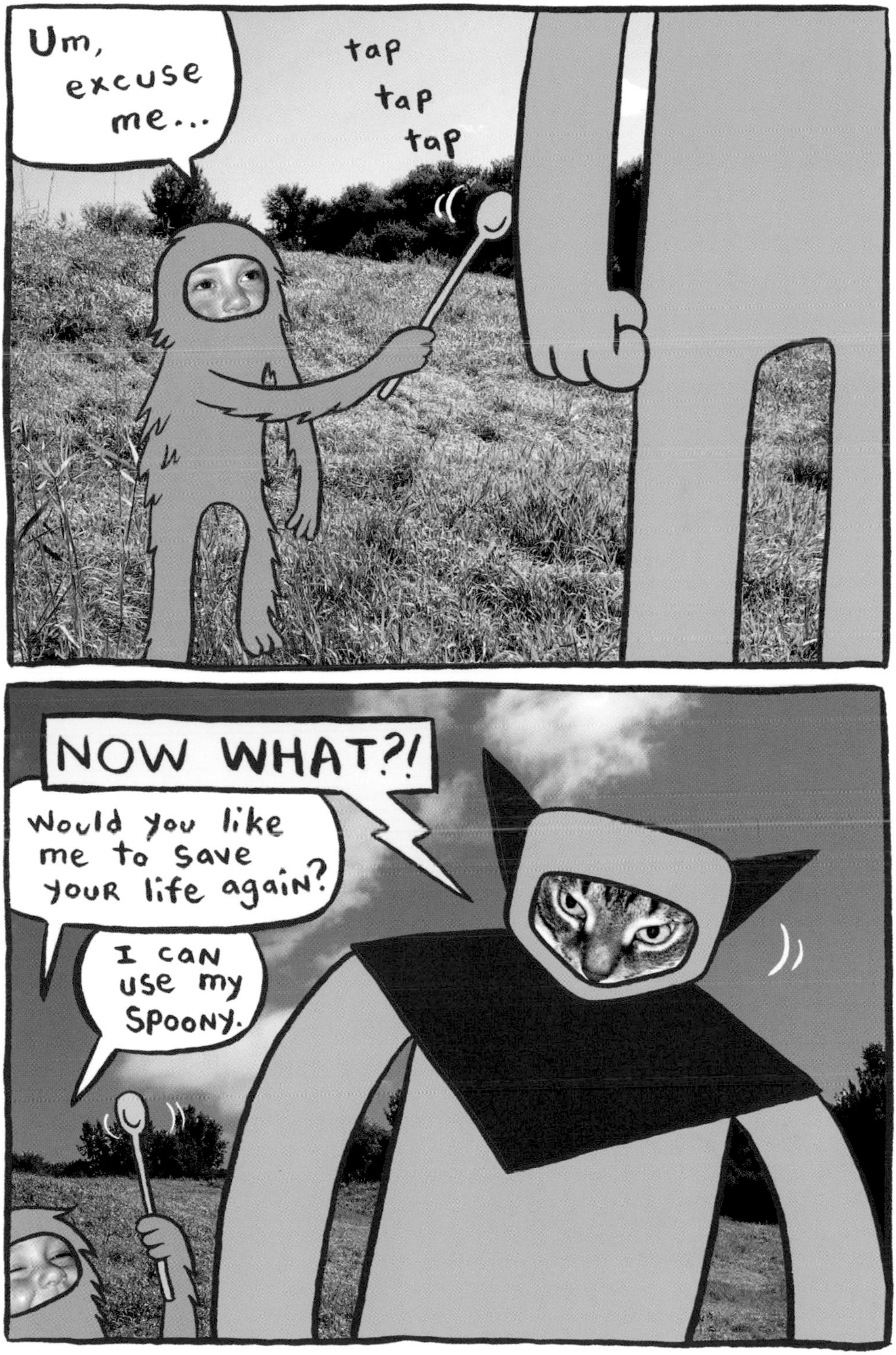
Um, excuse me...
tap tap tap
NOW WHAT?!
Would you like me to save your life again?
I can use my Spoony.

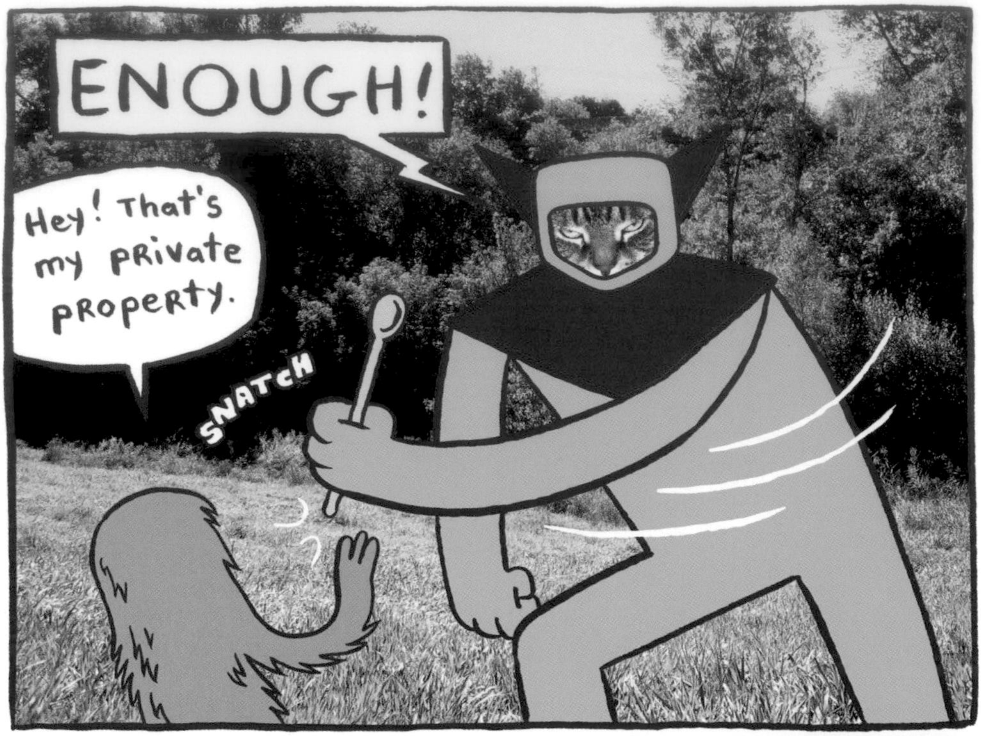
ENOUGH!
Hey! That's my private property.
SNATCH

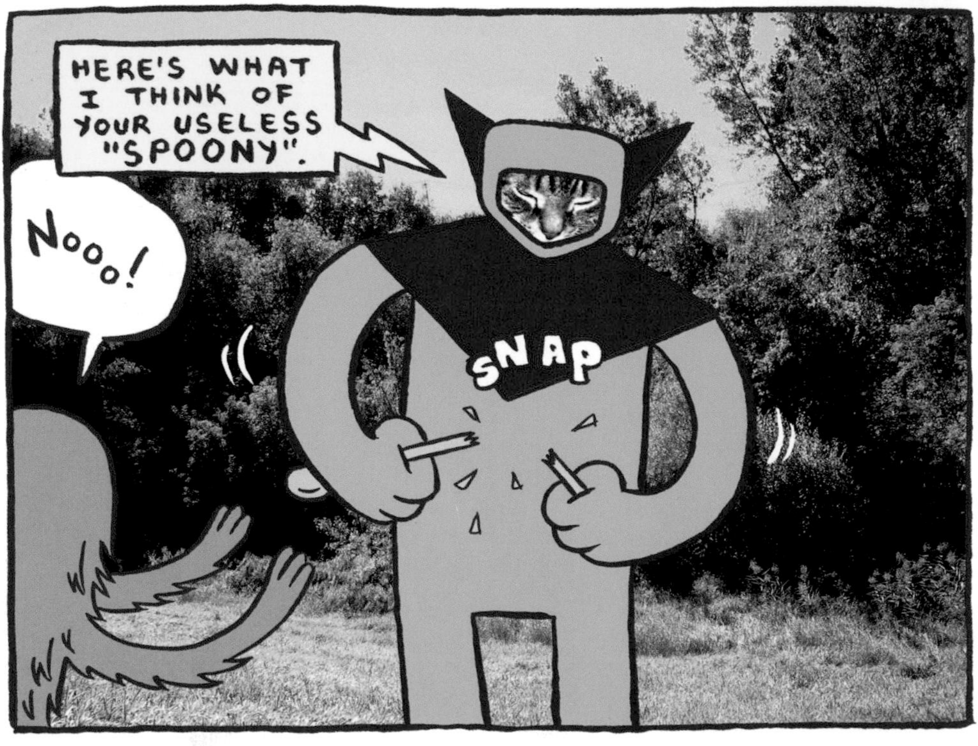
HERE'S WHAT I THINK OF YOUR USELESS "SPOONY".
Nooo!
SNAP

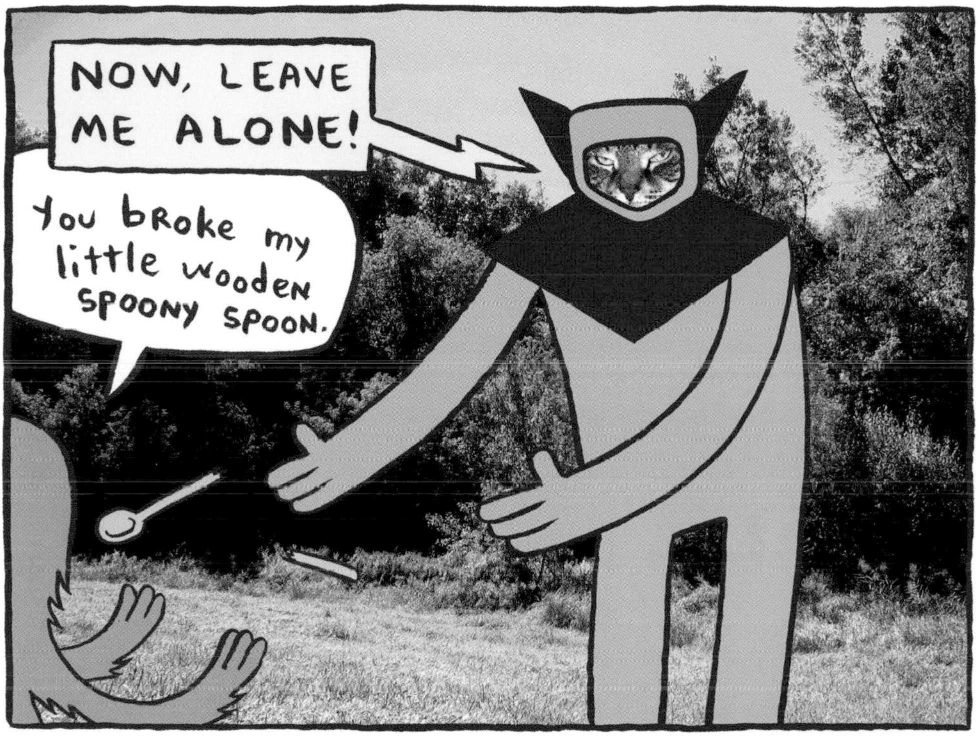
NOW, LEAVE ME ALONE!
You broke my little wooden spoony spoon.

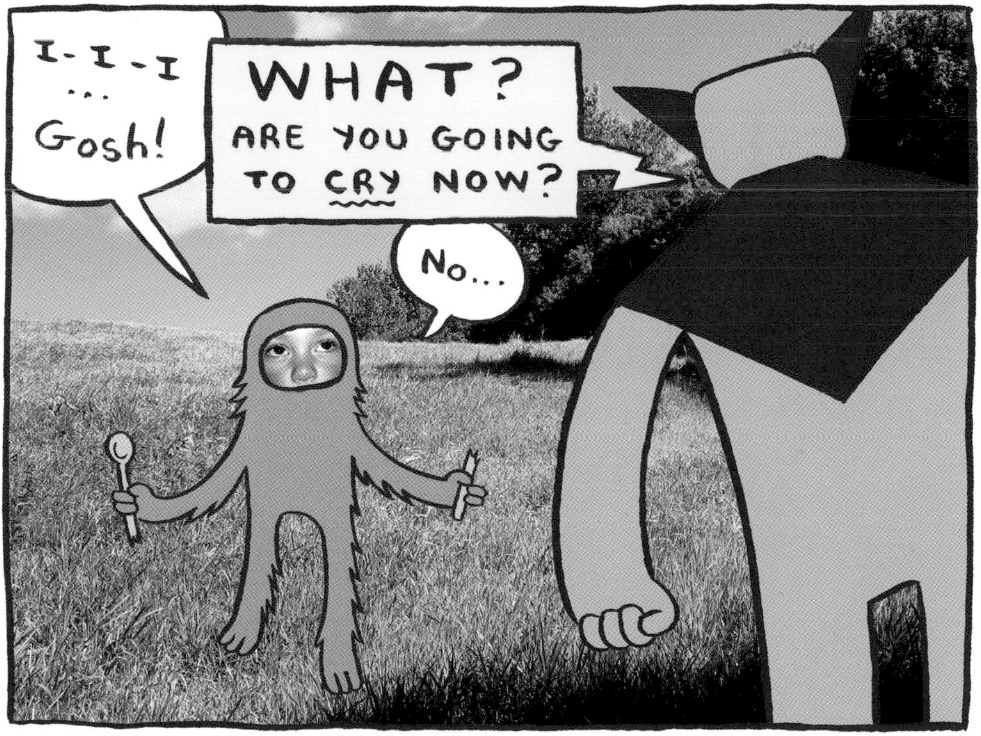
I-I-I ... Gosh!
WHAT? ARE YOU GOING TO CRY NOW?
No...

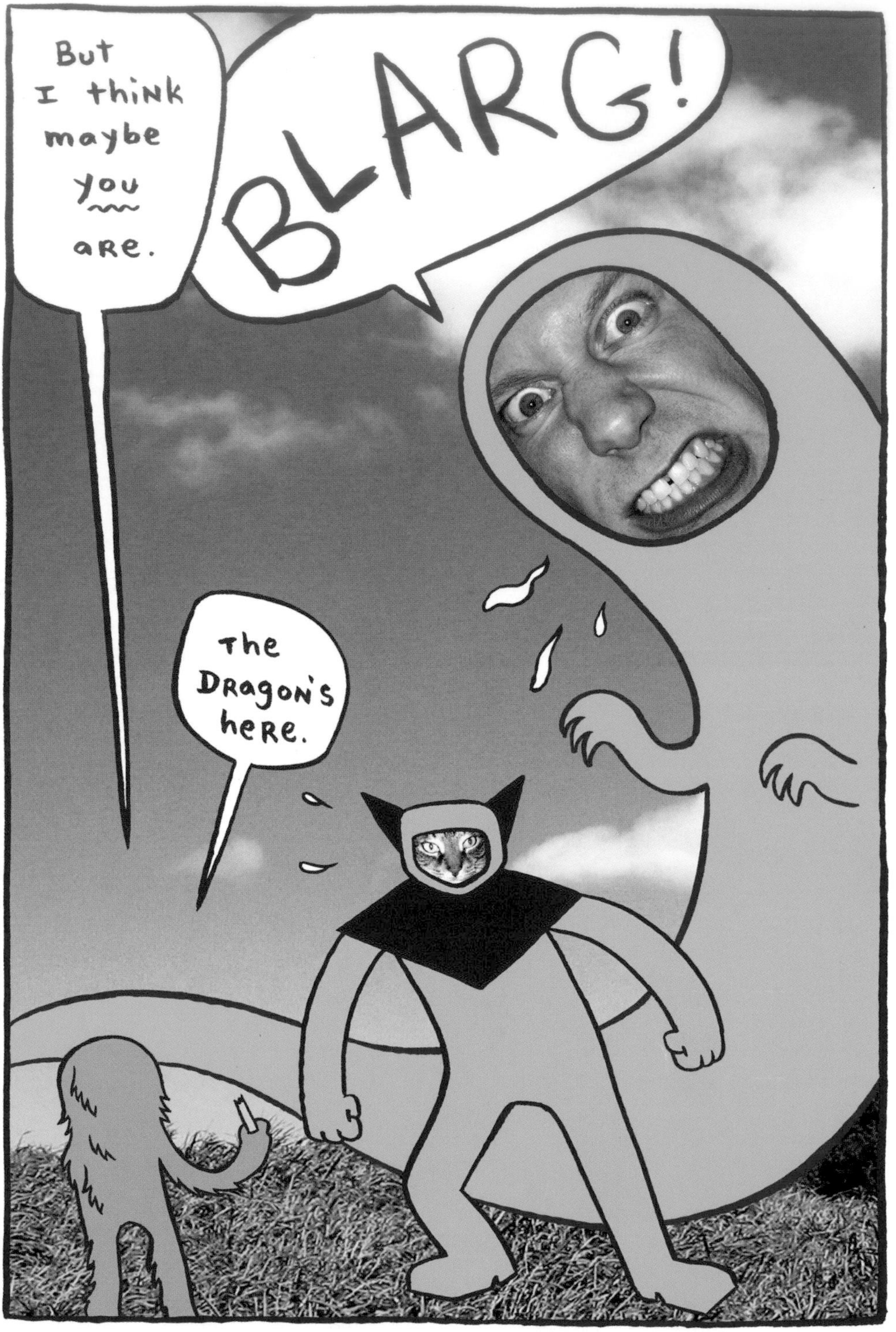
But I think maybe you are.
BLARG!
The Dragon's here.

CHAPTER THREE:

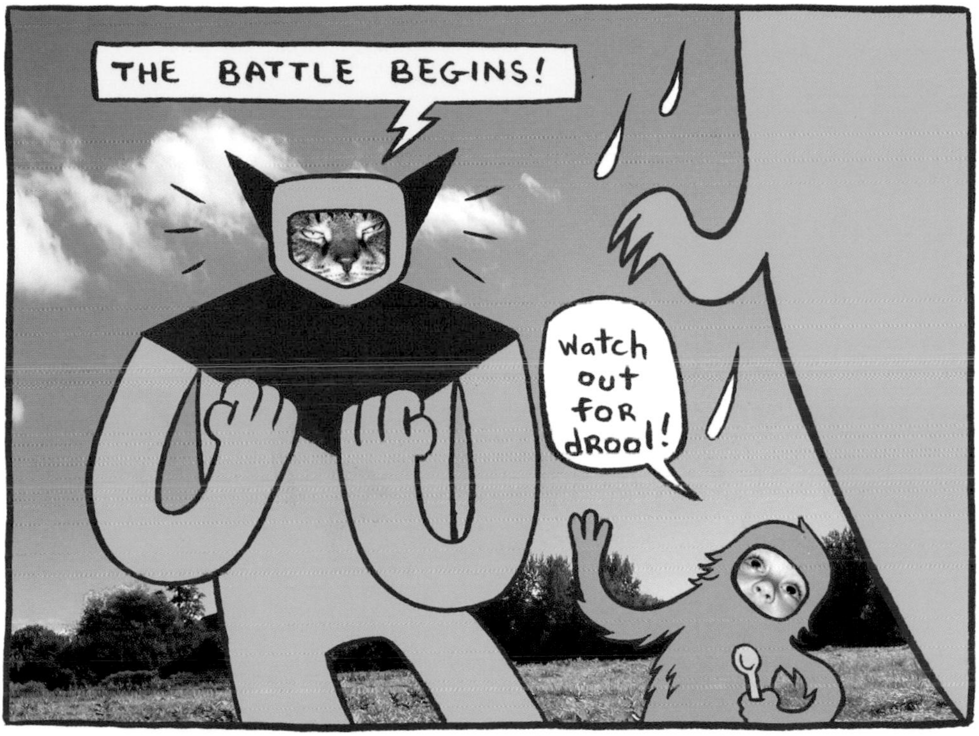
THE BATTLE BEGINS!
Watch out for drool!

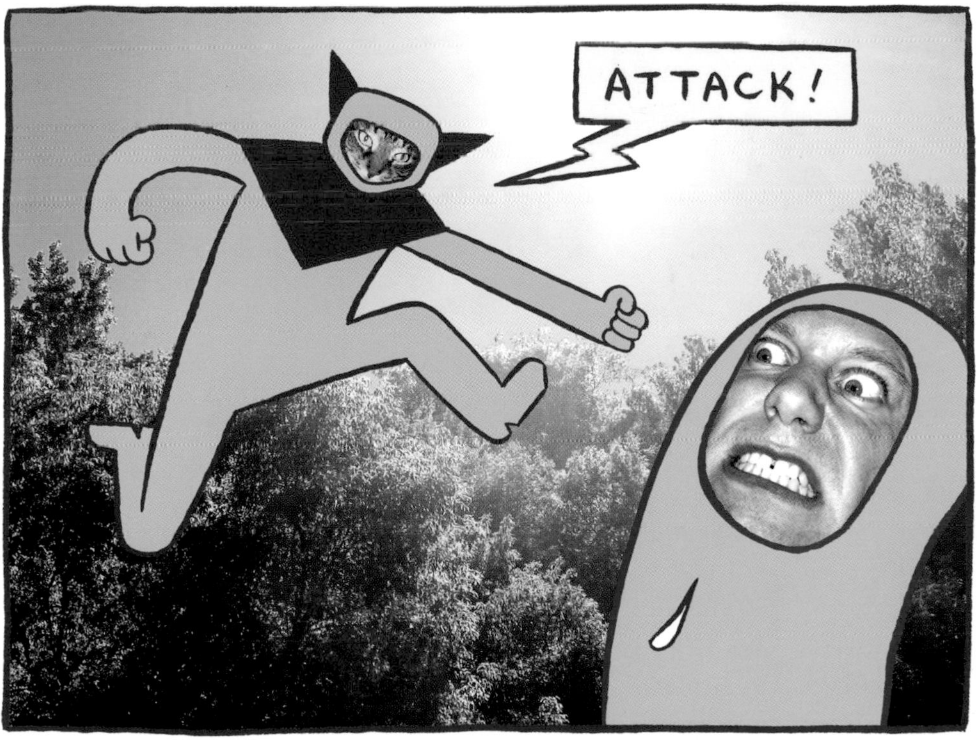
ATTACK!

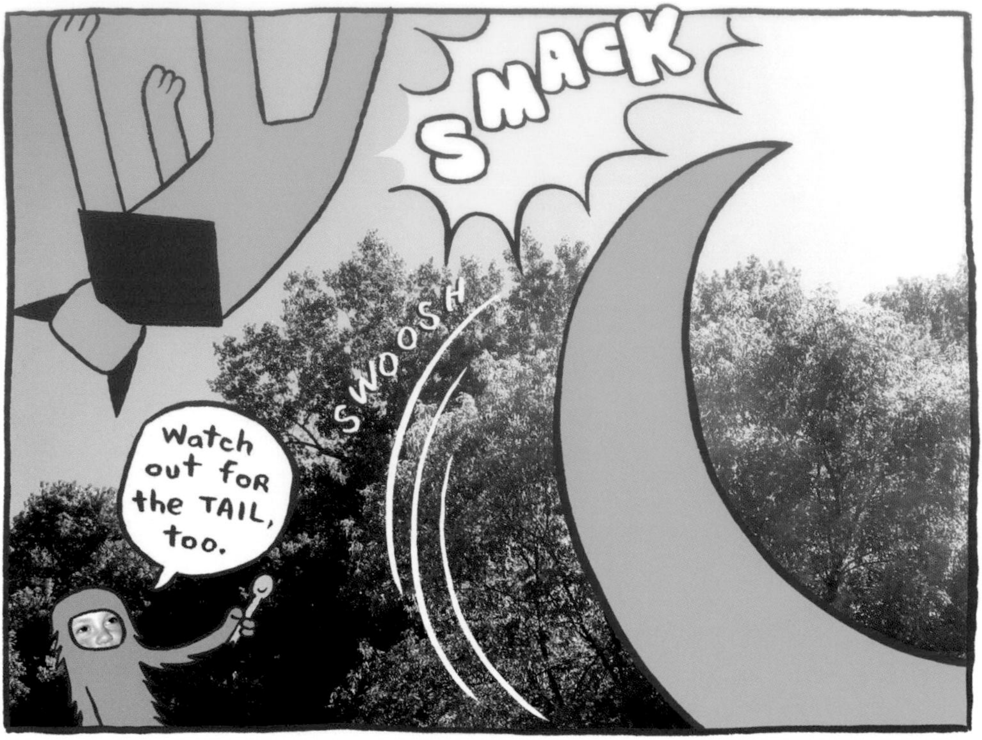
SMACK
SWOOSH
Watch out for the TAIL, too.

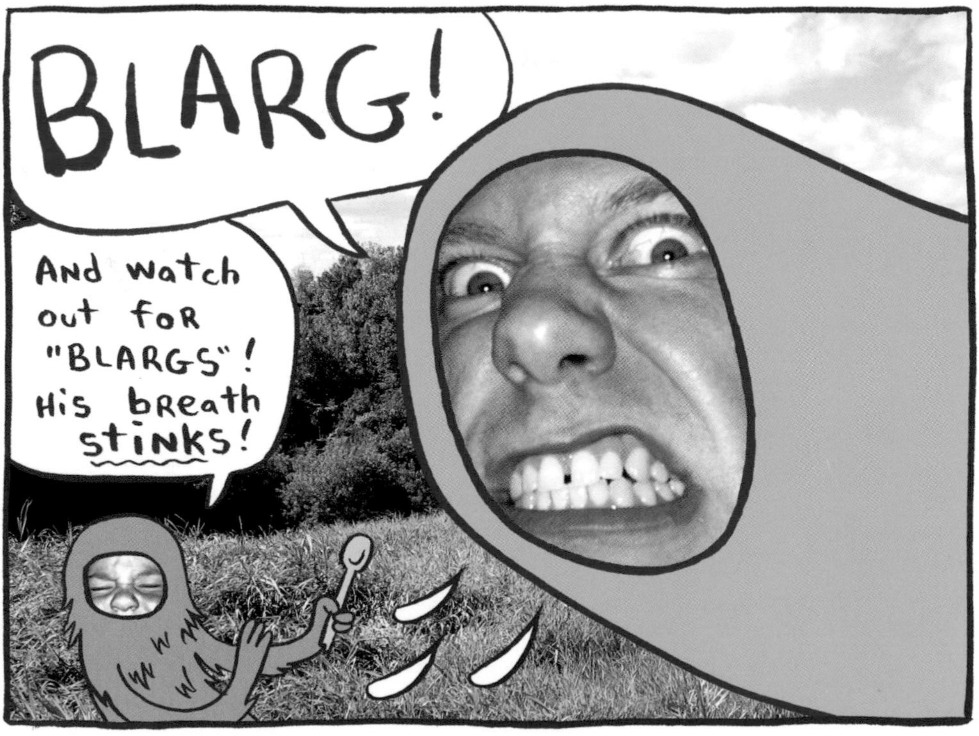
BLARG!
And watch out for "BLARGS"! His breath stinks!

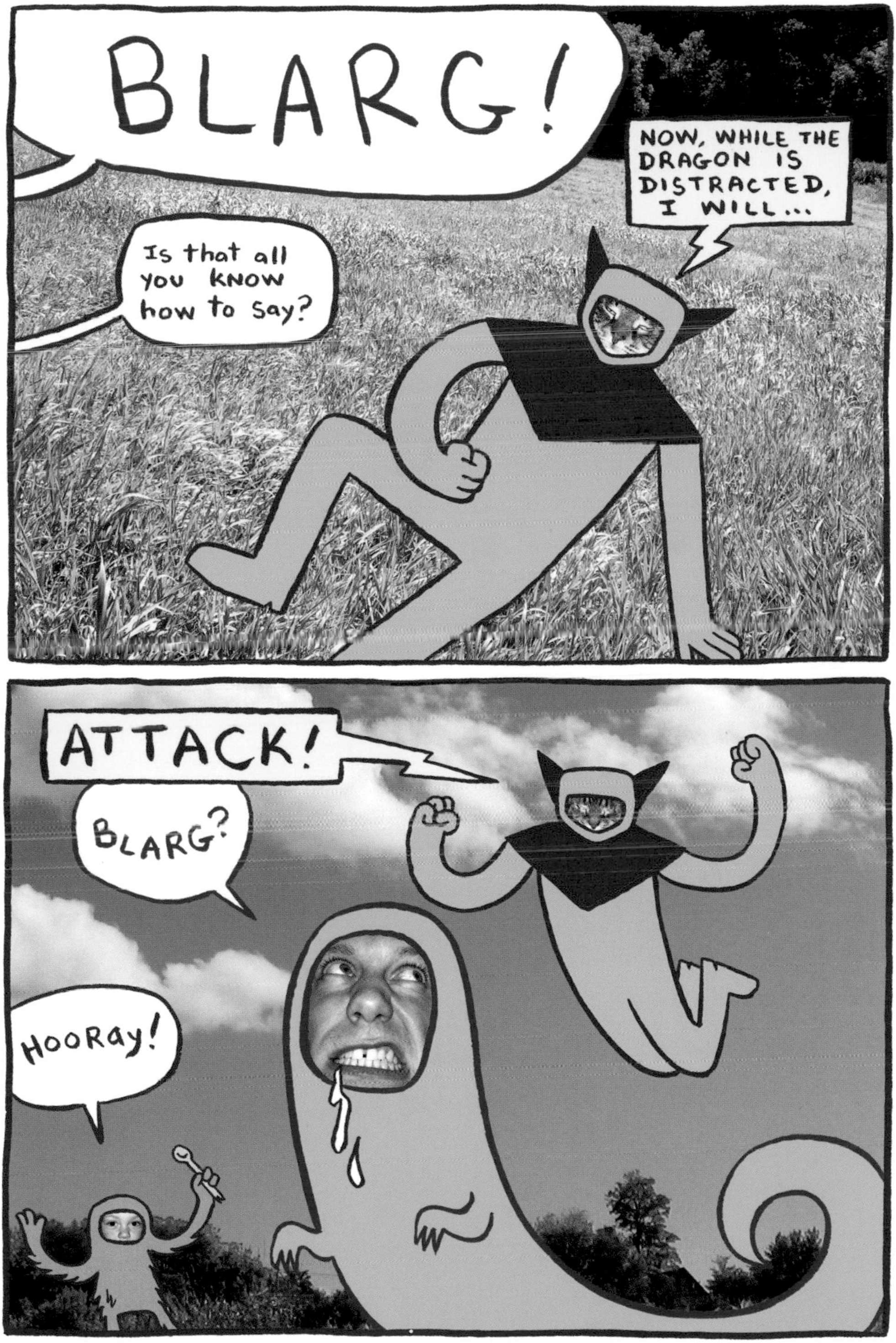
BLARG!
NOW, WHILE THE DRAGON IS DISTRACTED, I WILL...
Is that all you KNOW how to say?
ATTACK!
BLARG?
HOORAY!

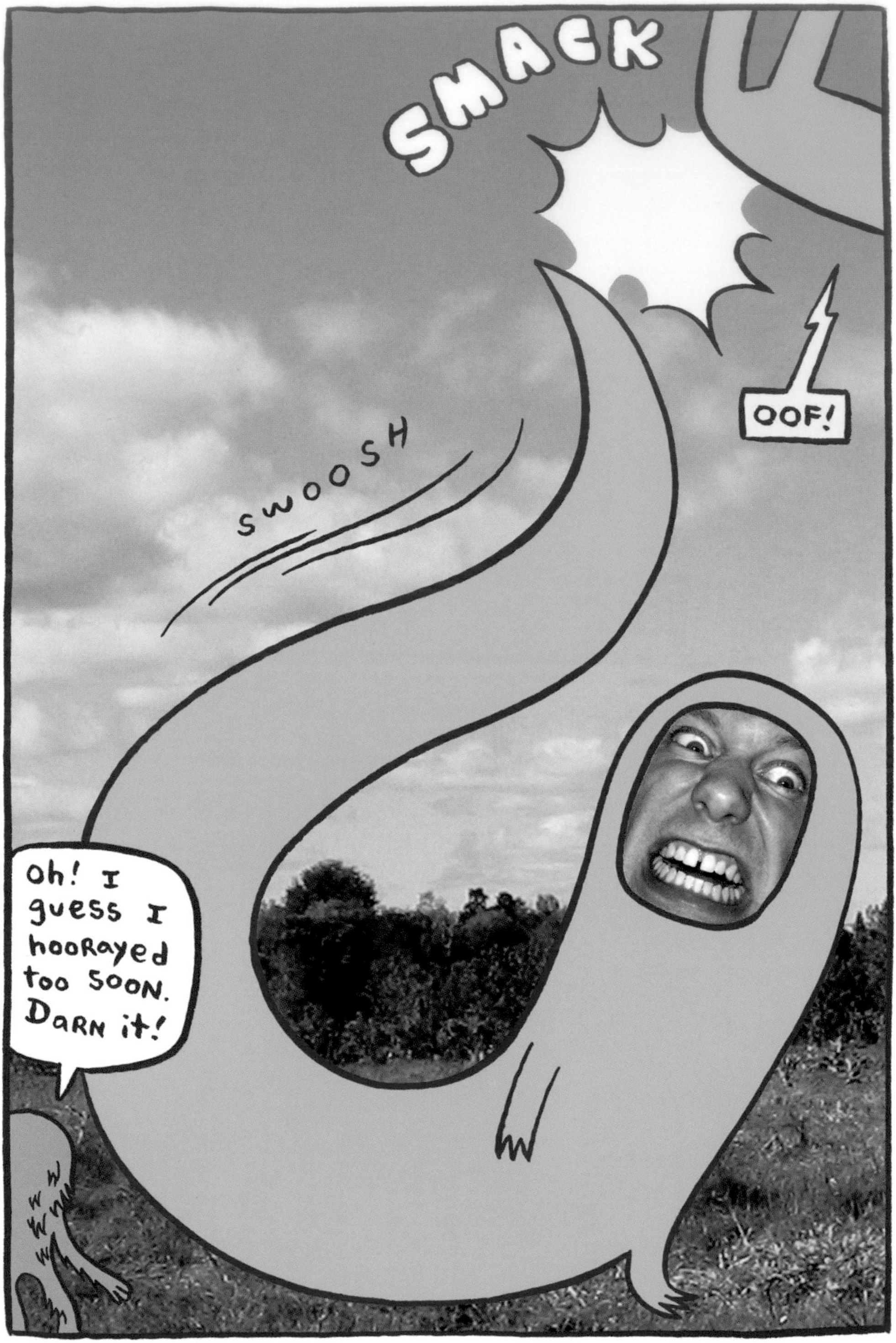
SMACK
OOF!
SWOOSH
Oh! I guess I hoorayed too soon. Darn it!

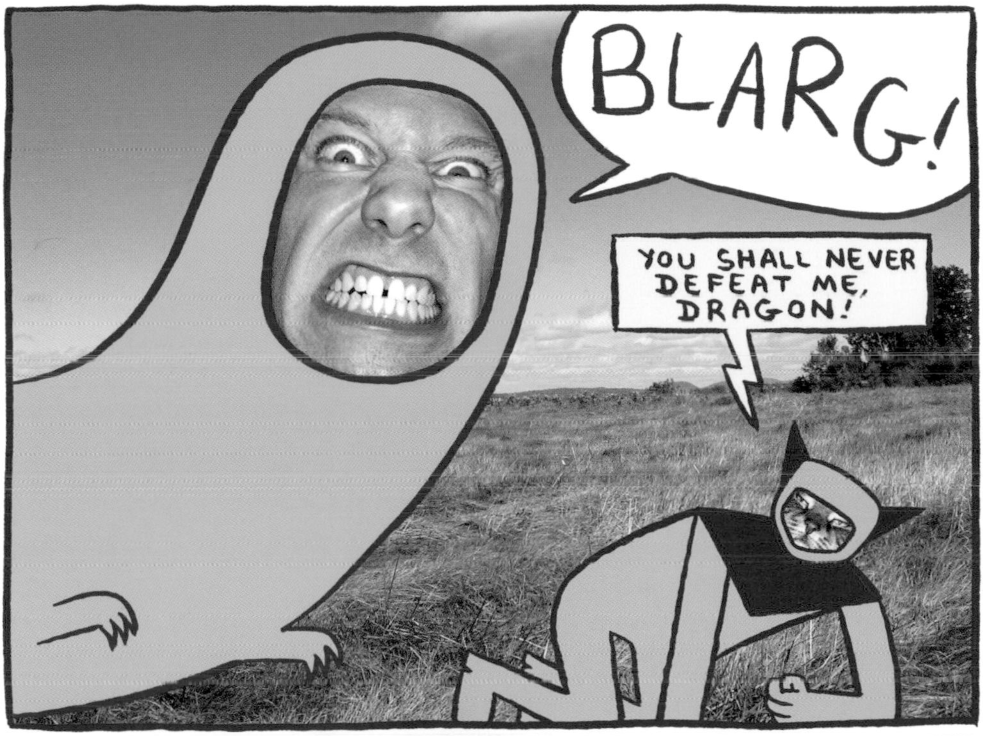
BLARG!
YOU SHALL NEVER DEFEAT ME, DRAGON!

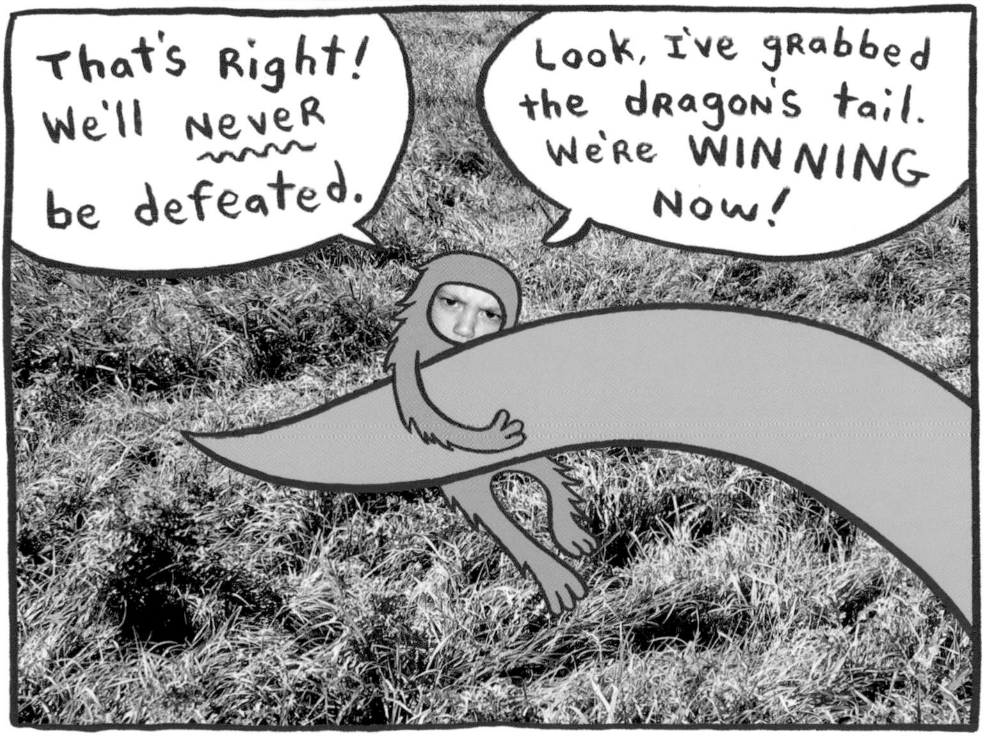
That's Right! We'll NeveR be defeated.
Look, I've grabbed the dragon's tail. We're WINNING Now!

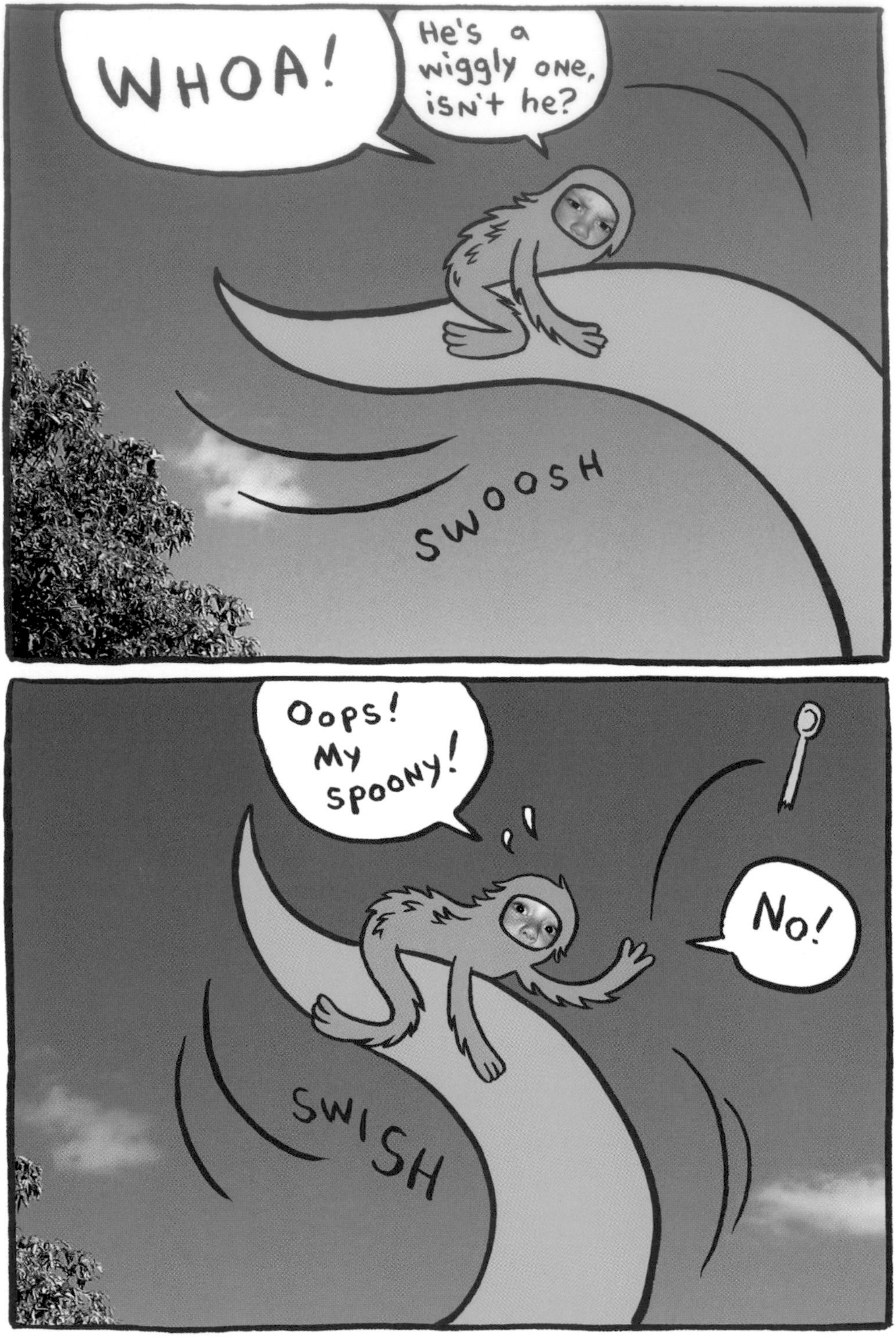
WHOA!
He's a wiggly one, isn't he?
SWOOSH
Oops! My spoony!
No!
SWISH

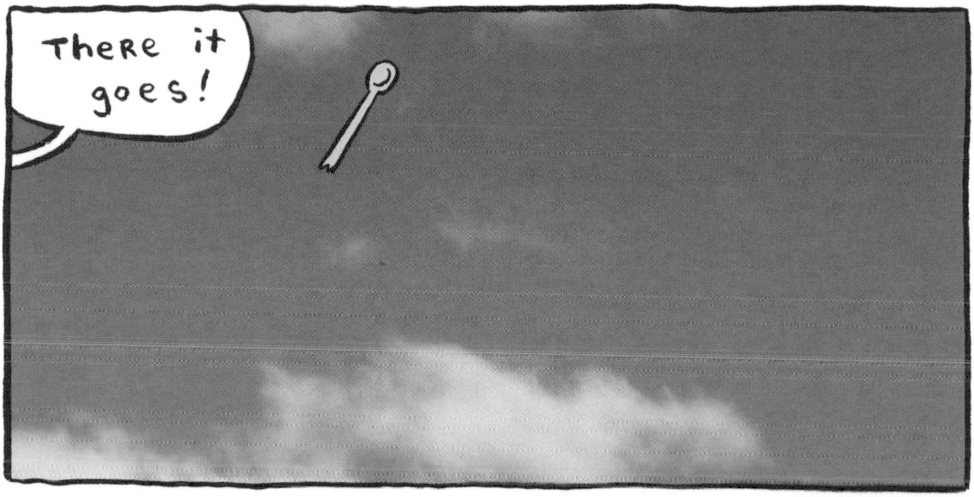
There it goes!

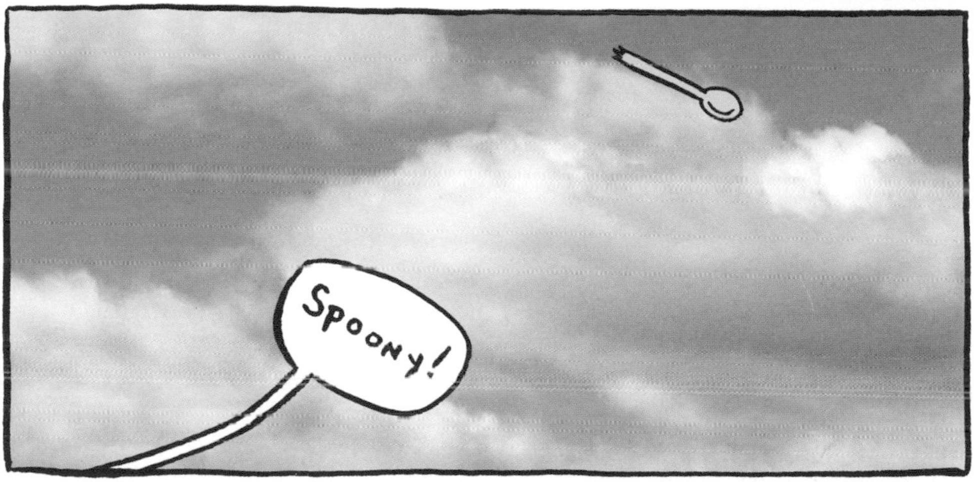
Spoony!

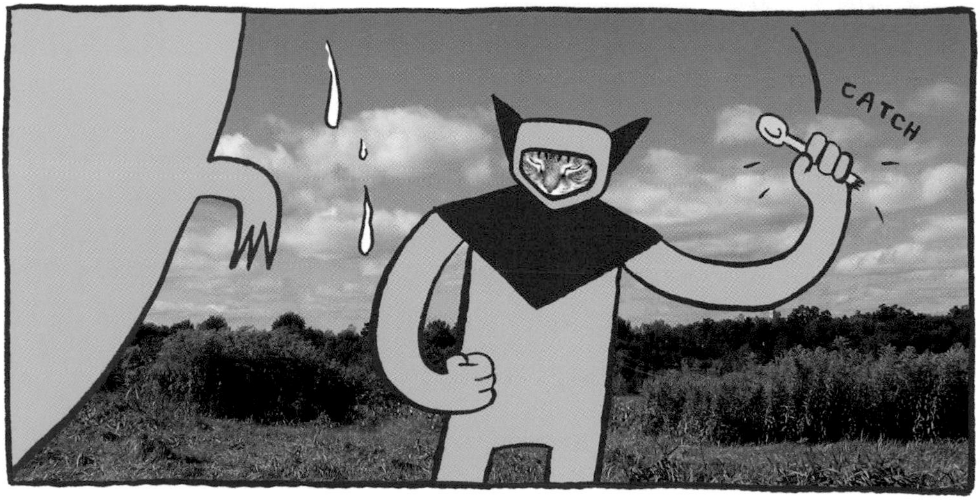
CATCH

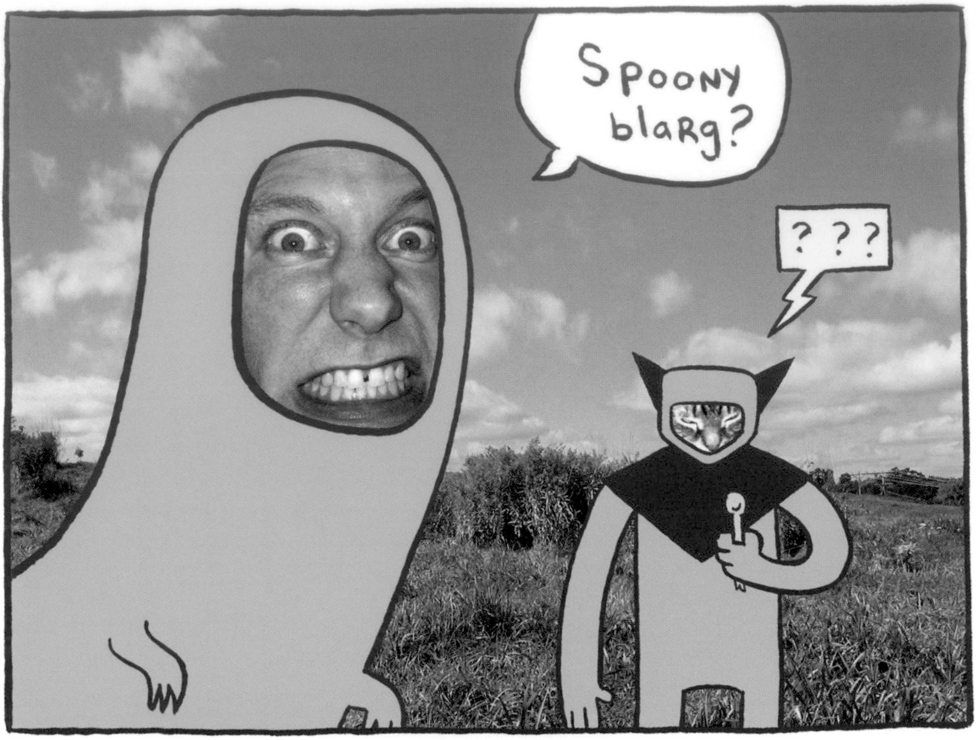
Spoony blarg?
???

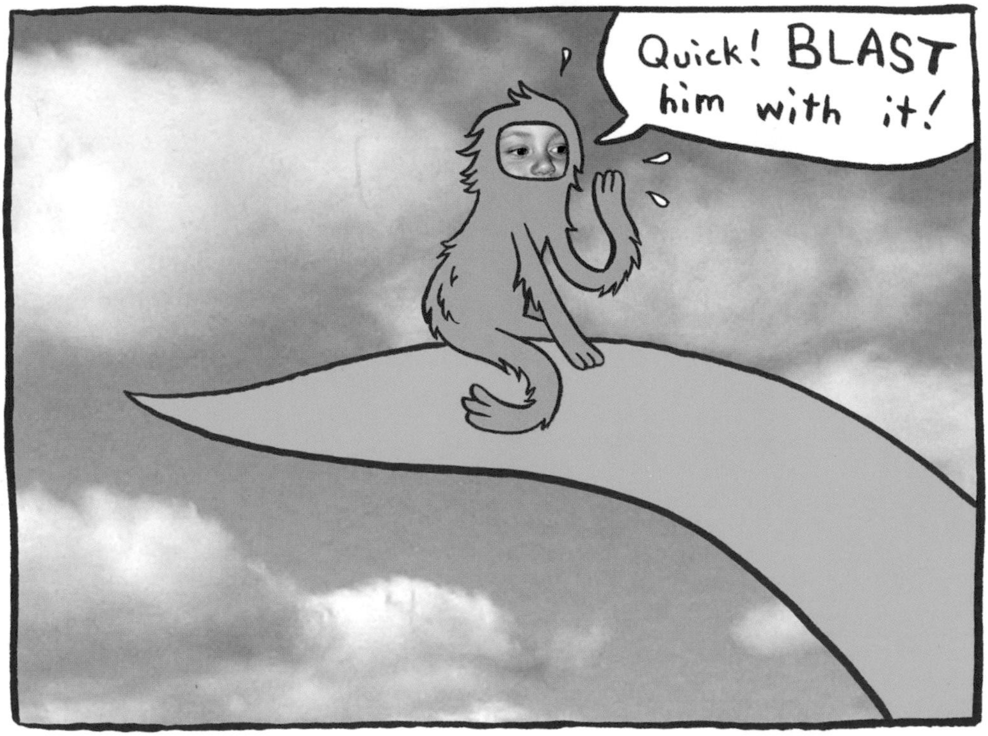
Quick! BLAST him with it!

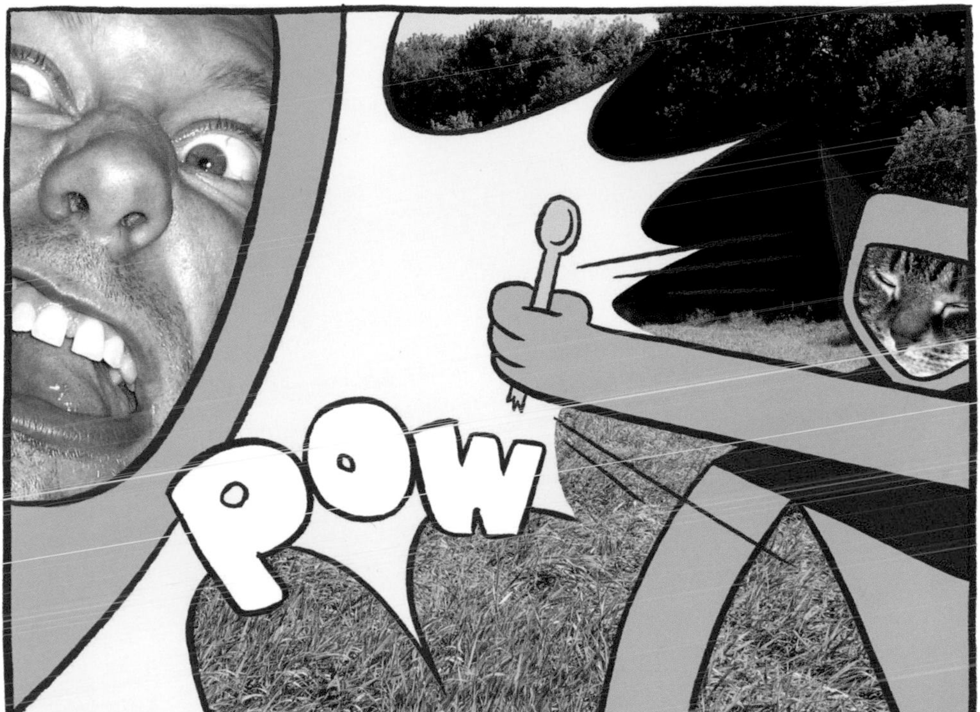
POW

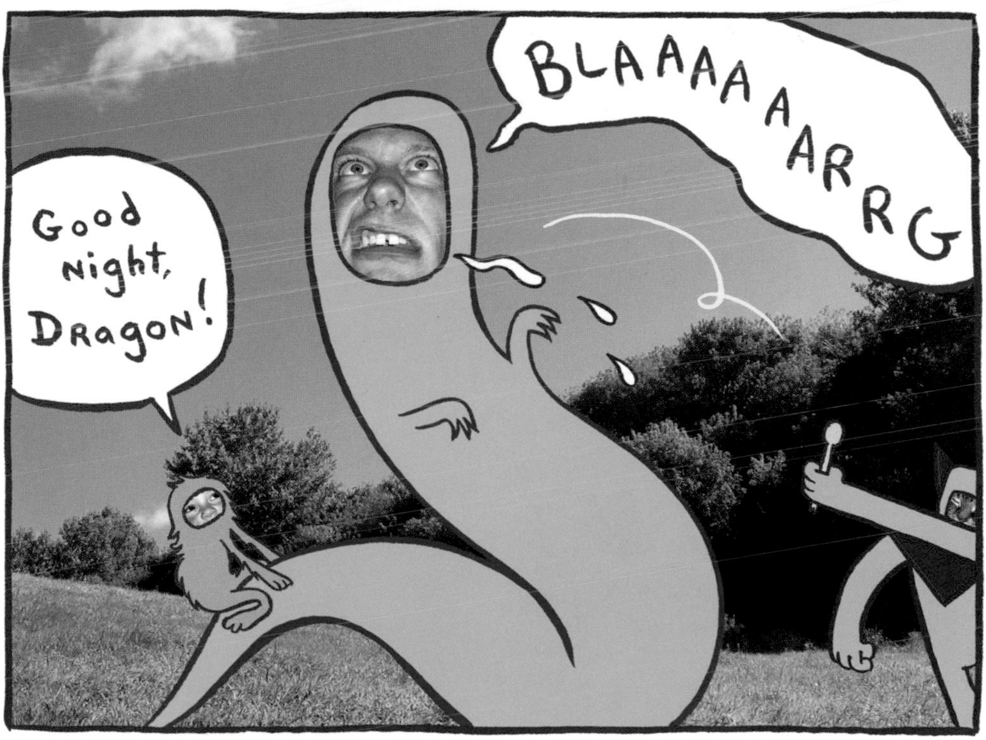
BLAAAAAARRG
Good night, Dragon!

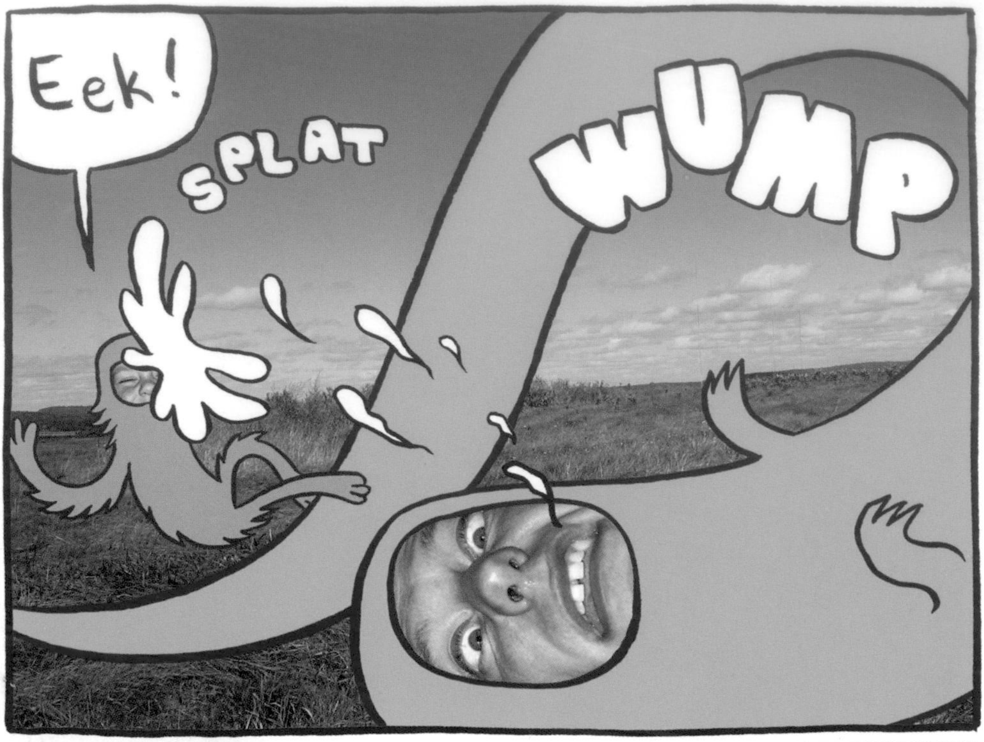
Eek!
SPLAT
WUMP
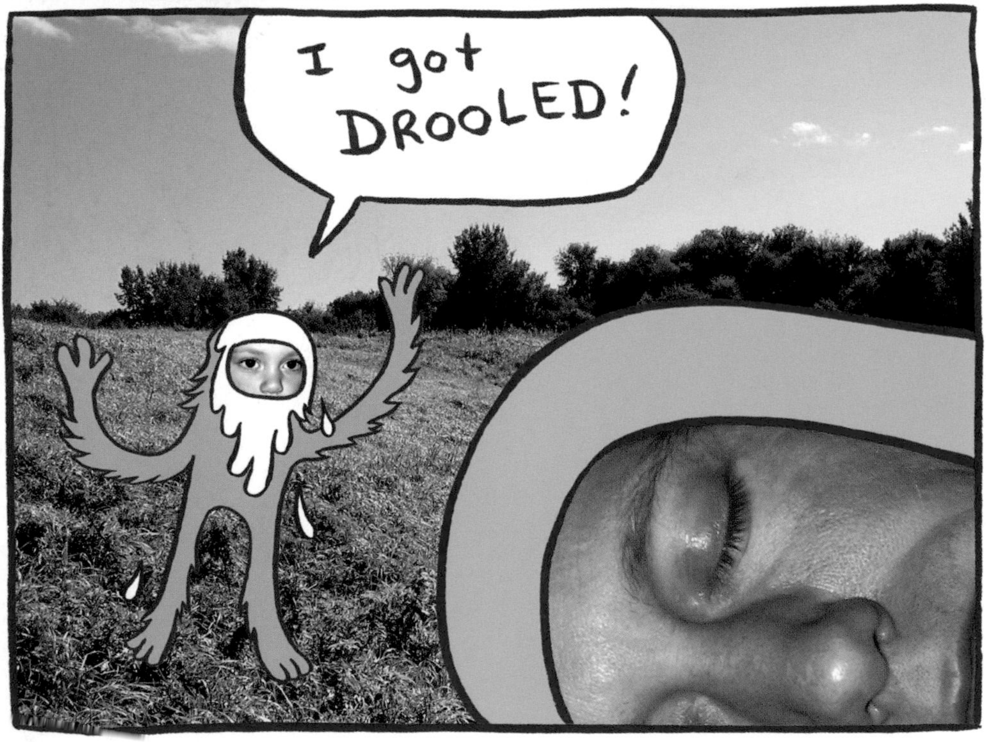
I got DROOLED!

EPILOGUE:

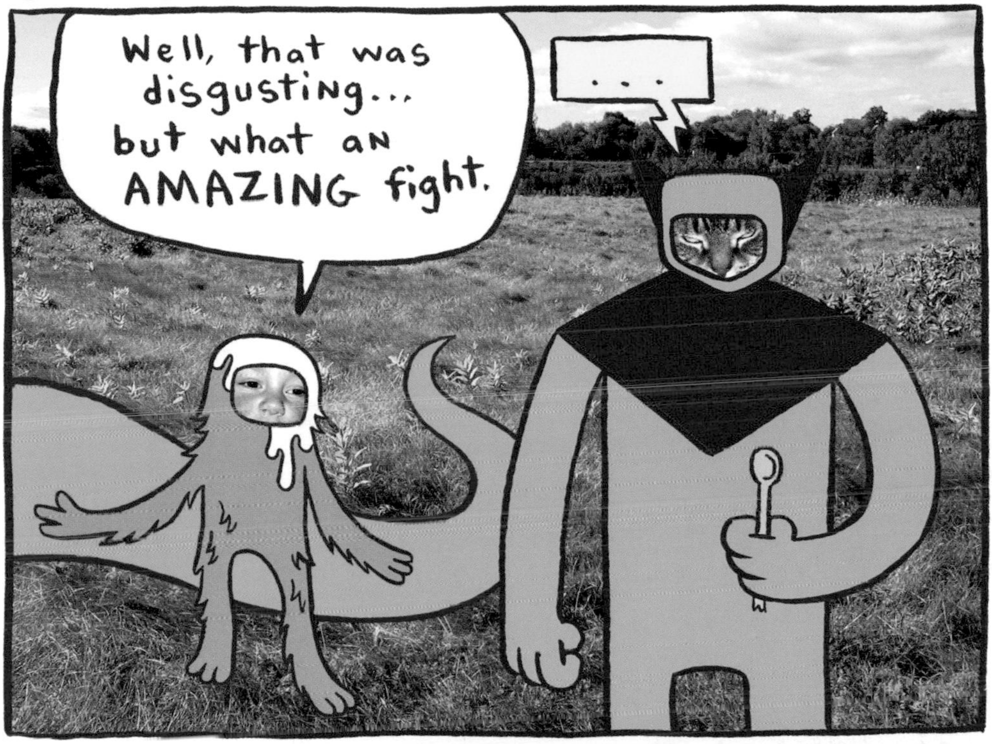

Well, that was disgusting... but what an AMAZING fight.
...

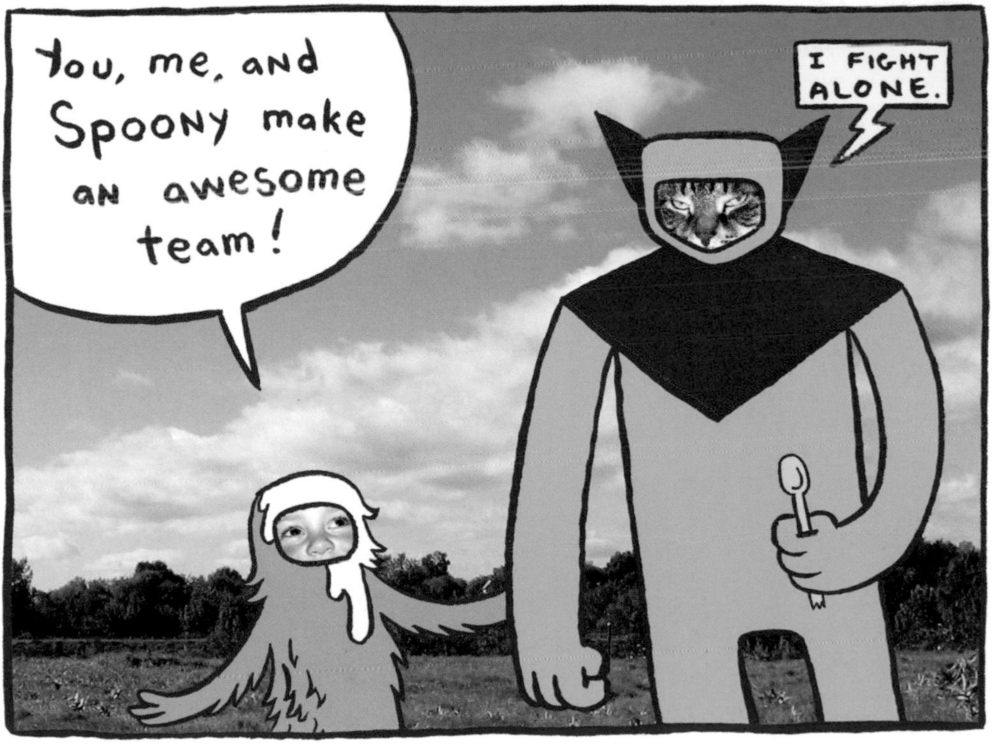

You, me, and Spoony make an awesome team!
I FIGHT ALONE.

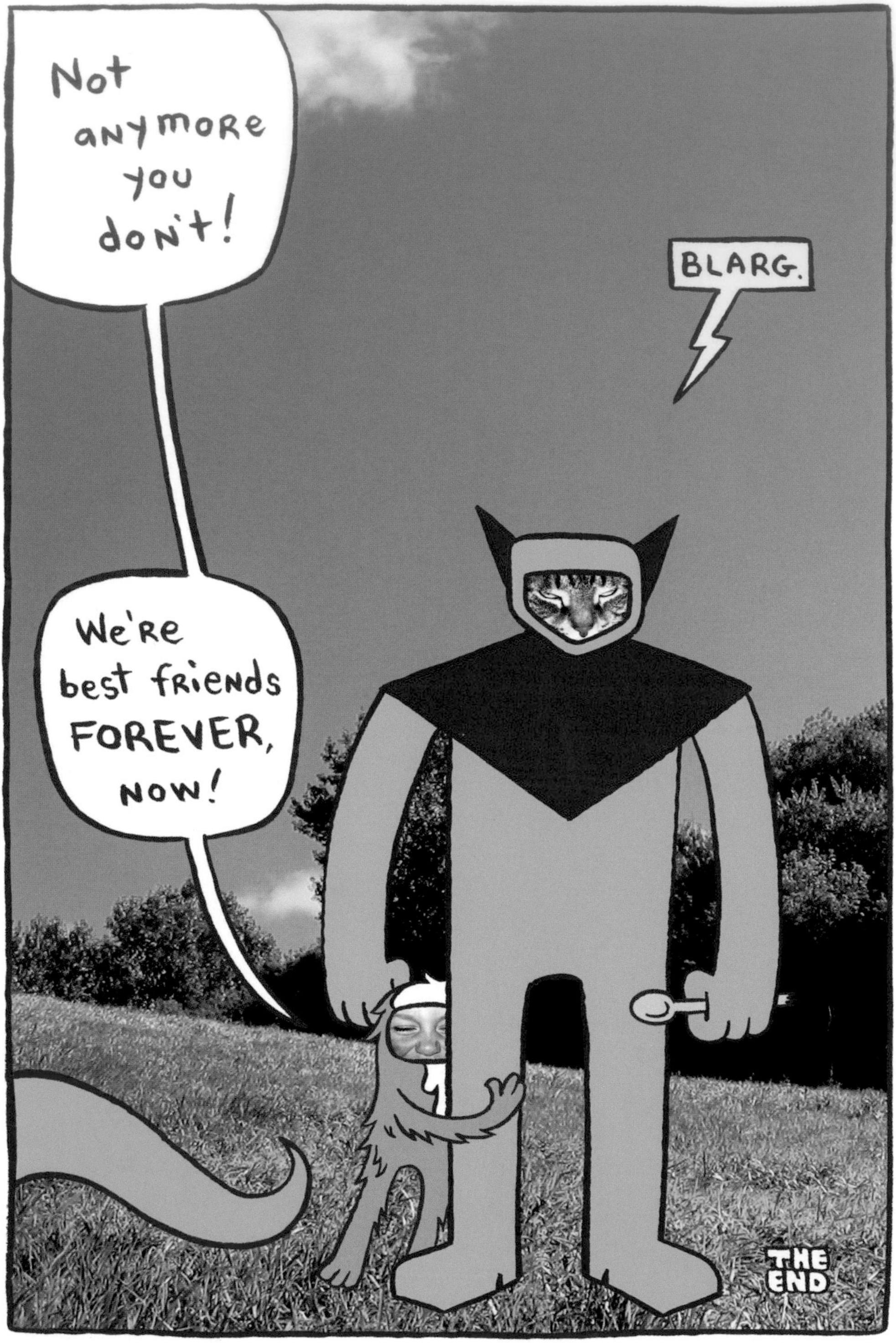
Not anymore you don't!
BLARG.
We're best friends FOREVER, now!
THE END

STARRING:

SPANDY as the DRAGON PUNCHER. Spandy is the author's pet cat and she has quite the temper! She likes to hiss at children.

ELI KOCHALKA as SPOONY-E. Eli posed for the pictures in this book when he was only 3 years old. He's older NOW. When he was a baby, he loved spoons.

JAMES KOCHALKA as the DRAGON. James is not only Eli's father, he's also the artist and author of this book.

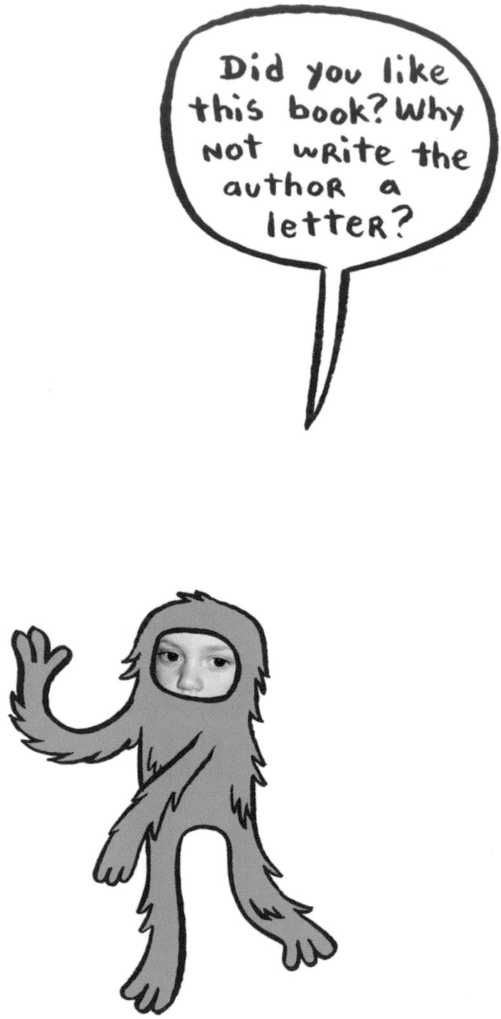
Did you like this book? Why not write the author a letter?

James Kochalka
P.O. Box 8321
Burlington, VT
05402

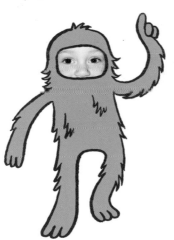

Now quick, Read the book again!

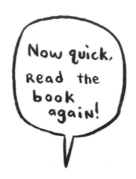

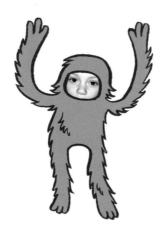